"You and I were friends, and you are back, and it's high time we opened those closet doors, don't you think? So. Dinner," Ryder repeated. *"Just you and me."*

"And if I say no?"

"I'm not above kidnapping you."

"I don't know, Ry. Could I at least think about it?"

"Of course."

And that should have been his cue to haul his sorry ass through the door and out to his car. If he'd been inclined, that is, to listen to his head and not whatever made him instead lift one hand to brush his thumb across her rapidly cooling cheek, a move that sent his stomach into a freefall.

Mel sucked in a breath, her eyes going even bigger. "What the hell are you doing?"

"Seriously thinking about things I've got no right to think about."

Dear Reader,

It always amazes me how often the tiniest seed of inspiration can grow into a whole story. Or, as with Summer Sisters, an entire series. In this case I'm talking memories of childhood vacations spent in North Carolina with my two close-in-age cousins, when my father would take me to visit my grandmother nearly every summer. I still remember long, jostling rides in the back of somebody's Country Squire station wagon, cannonballing into assorted swimming pools and jamming out to the Beach Boys (guess that decade!).

Of course, this is fiction, and my cousins and I aren't anything like Mel, April and Blythe. High Point, North Carolina, turned into make-believe St. Mary's Cove on Maryland's eastern shore, and heaven knows none of us went on to lead lives anywhere near as tangled in secrets as those three. But the love and camaraderie, the shared silliness and laughter—those, the six of us had in common. Like all three of my heroines, I, too, was an only child, who cherished those weeks every summer when I had "sisters." And writing these stories has allowed me to pay tribute to those gals…and those wonderful memories.

Enjoy!

Karen Templeton

THE DOCTOR'S DO-OVER

KAREN TEMPLETON

HARLEQUIN®
entertain, enrich, inspire™

Recycling programs
for this product may
not exist in your area.

ISBN-13: 978-0-373-65693-6

THE DOCTOR'S DO-OVER

www.Harlequin.com

Printed in U.S.A.

KAREN TEMPLETON

Since 1998, two-time RITA® Award winner and Waldenbooks bestselling author Karen Templeton has written more than thirty novels for Harlequin Books. A transplanted Easterner, she now lives in New Mexico with two hideously spoiled cats and whichever of her five sons happens to be in residence.

To Amy and Lainey
Here's to memories of hot summers,
frigid swimming pools,
sighing over boys
and more good times than I can count.
Miss you guys.

Chapter One

Her nostrils twitching at the putrid mix of mildew, ancient grease and whatever it was that had died in her grandmother's Nixon-era refrigerator, Melanie Duncan could only gawk in horrified amazement. Holy cannoli—Amelia Rinehart had apparently kept every glass jar and plastic container she'd ever touched.

Along with—shuddering, Mel thunked shut the grimy, mustard-yellow cabinet door—decades' worth of magazines, newspapers and junk mail stacked in teetering piles throughout the eight-freaking-bedroom house. And just think, she thought sourly, shoving up the nasty water faucet with her wrist and waiting for-*ev*-er for the hot water to meander up from the basement, it was all hers. Hers and April's and Blythe's, that is.

With that, her gaze also meandered, out the dirt-fogged window and beyond the weed-infested backyard sloping down to the inlet beyond, to the slate blue water glitter-

ing in the late September sunshine…and she could almost
see those three girls sunbathing on the pier, stretched out
on Walmart-issue beach towels as Green Day blared from
somebody's old boom box. Blythe's, most likely.

The water suddenly went blistering hot, making Mel
yelp. Cursing, she adjusted the handle, thinking maybe
she was still in shock. Not so much about her grandmother's passing—she had been nearly ninety, after all, even
if Death probably had to hog-tie her and drag her away
kicking and screaming. But, yeah, inheriting the Eastern
Shore property, especially since her grandmother and she
hadn't spoken in more than ten years? That was strange.
Far more strange than that, however, was finding herself
in the last place she'd ever expected to set foot again.

Or wanted to.

Anxiety prickling her chilled skin—the thermostat
didn't appear to be working—Mel scrubbed her hands with
the dish soap still sitting on the back of the pock-marked
sink and turned, only to grimace at the M. C. Escher-like
towers of long-since-expired bottles of herbal supplements
smothering the chipped Formica counters…the jungle of
dead plants at the base of the patio doors leading to the
disintegrating back porch…what appeared to be hundreds
of paper bags, undoubtedly loaded with mouse droppings,
wadded between the fridge and the cabinets. Dis*gust*ing,
as her daughter would say. Thank God the washing ma-
chine was working—go, Maytag—because no way in hell
was she letting her child sleep on any of the musty sheets
she'd found all jumbled up in the linen closet.

Had her grandmother always been that much of a pack-
rat? Or had the three of them turned blind eyes to the clutter during those long, lazy summers when the world as
they all knew it simply didn't exist?

Shaking her head, Mel tromped to the dining room and

yelled for her daughter, who, being made of sterner stuff than Mel, had gasped in utter delight the moment they'd set foot inside, then immediately taken off to explore.

"Quinn! Where are you?" she bellowed again, fighting images of the child fending off a posse of rats, breathing a sigh of relief at Quinn's faint, but strong, "Coming!" in reply.

She glowered at the behemoth of a buffet across the room, the blotchy mirror behind it nearly obliterated by more…stuff. Doodads and knickknacks and tchotchkes galore. And in every corner, packages of all shapes and sizes—some unopened, even—from every purveyor of useless crap on the planet.

So much for a quick in-and-out. What had clearly taken years to accumulate wasn't going to simply go *poof* in a couple of days. And then what? What the hell were the three of them supposed to do with the place? Yes, St. Mary's Cove was picturesque and all, but even divested of all the *stuff,* potential buyers would take one look and laugh their tushies off. And she sincerely doubted that either of her cousins had the funds, let alone the where-withal, to fix it up. She sure as hell didn't, a thought that only shoved Mel back down into the Pit of Despair she'd been trying—with scant success—to climb out of for what felt like forever.

With a mighty sigh, she hiked through the House of Horrors and outside to her trusty little Honda to unload the backseat, the tangy, slightly fruity bay breeze catching her off guard. Oh, no. Not doing nostalgia, nope.

And just like that, there he was. In her head, of course, not in person, since there was no reason for him to know she was even here—and God willing, that's how this little episode would play out—but…damn.

She hadn't allowed herself to think of him in years.

Had almost convinced herself it didn't matter anymore. *He* didn't matter anymore, that what they'd shared was as firmly and irrevocably in the past as those long ago summers—

"Mom? Whatcha doing?"

Mel glanced up, smiling for the slightly frowning ten-year-old—her life, her love, her reason for living—standing on the porch, all turn-of-the-century charm fallen on hard times, and her heart turned over in her chest. Heaven knows she'd made a boatload of mistakes in her life— oh, let her count the ways—but the skinny fifth-grader with the wild red hair currently standing with her hands planted on her skinny, not-at-all-like-Mama's, hips wasn't one of them.

Although the circumstances of her conception? In a class by itself.

"Unpacking. And good news! You can come play pack mule." Because there was no way she was leaving that half-finished cheesecake to rot back in Baltimore while they were here. Or the pumpkin soufflé. Or the...

Okay, she liked her own cooking. So sue her.

They carted the various Tupperwared goodies into the kitchen, at which point Quinn gasped, bug-eyed, then shook her head."Looks like you and me have got some *serious* cleaning to do."

"You might say," Mel said as she cautiously opened the doors under the sink to find—booyah!—six half-empty containers of Comet and as many boxes of garbage bags, a bucketload of desiccated sponges and enough Lysol to disinfect a cruise ship. And, praise be, two un-opened packages of rubber gloves. *The good Lord will provide*, she heard her mother say, and tears threatened. *Not going there, either,* Mel thought, standing and handing her daughter a pair of gloves, a sponge and one of the Comets.

"Start with the sink." Gloves donned, Mel yanked out a garbage bag and faced the fridge. "This puppy is *mine*."

"Got it." Quinn dragged over a step stool to better reach inside the sink, wriggled into her own gloves and got to it, determination oozing from every pore in her little body... as she started to sing, loudly and very badly, a song from *Wicked*.

What a little weirdo, Mel thought, chuckling. A little weirdo, she thought on a sharp intake of breath, she'd protect with everything she had in her.

Especially from people who wanted to pretend she didn't exist.

Looking up from Jenny O'Hearn's chart, Ryder Caldwell stared at his father's white-coated back, the words barely registering.

"What did you say?"

David Caldwell slid his pen back into his top pocket, then directed a steady, but concerned, gaze at Ryder before removing the coat and snagging it onto a hook on the back of his office door. "That Amelia left the house to the girls."

Not that this was any surprise, Ryder thought over the pinching inside his chest as he watched his dad shrug into the same tan corduroy sport coat he wore to work every day, rain or shine—much to Ryder's mother's annoyance— then yank down the cuffs of his blue Oxford shirt. Made perfect sense, in fact, Amelia Rinehart's bequeathing the house to the three cousins who'd spent, what? Nine or ten summers there? At least?

What was a surprise, was his reaction to the news. That after all this time the prospect of seeing Mel again should provoke any kind of reaction at all. After all, stuff happened. People grew up, moved on—

"You okay?"

Ryder glanced up at his father. Although David's lanky form stooped more than it used to, and silver riddled his thick, dark hair, it often startled Ryder that it was like seeing an age progression image of what Ryder himself would look like in thirty years. Unlike his younger brother Jeremy, who'd inherited their mother's fair skin and red hair. *Among other things*.

"Of course, why wouldn't I be?" he said, flipping closed Jenny's file, then striding down the short hall to the empty waiting room to leave it on Evelyn's desk to tend to the next morning. Outside, a light rain had begun to speckle the oversize windows of the small family practice clinic on Main Street his father had started nearly thirty years ago, where Ryder had joined him—again, much to his mother's annoyance—after completing his residency five years ago. The clinic, his practice, had been the only constants in a life clearly determined to knock him flat on his butt with irritating regularity. Good thing that butt was made of rubber, was all he had to say. "But how did you—"

"Golf. Phil," his father said behind him, rattling his keys. "Far as he knows they'll be here today or tomorrow. To decide what to do with the place." He paused. "Just thought you should know."

"Because of Mel?"

A slight smile curved his father's lips. "That little girl worshipped the ground you walked on. Never saw a pair of kids as close as you two were."

Slipping into a tan windbreaker nearly as old as his father's jacket, Ryder turned to the older man, now standing by the front door. "That was years ago, Dad," he said over the twist of guilt, an almost welcome change from the pain he still lugged around after nearly a year. "We haven't even spoken since that summer." Another twist. "After her father died—"

"There's a child, Ry."

Again, the words weren't making sense. How—why—
did his father know this? And what on earth did it have to
do with Ryder? "So she has a kid—"

"She's ten."

And that would be the sound of pieces slamming into
place. "And you think she's *mine?* Excuse me, Dad, but
that's not possible—"

"I know she's not yours, Ry," his father said wearily.
Bleakly. "She's your brother's."

His head still spinning, Ryder sat across the street from
the massive quasi-Victorian, set well back on its equally
massive, and woefully neglected, lot. He'd been there a
while, parked in the dark, dead space between the street
lamps and not giving a rat's ass that the damp from the now
full-out rain had seeped into his bones. He had no idea, of
course, if the little white Honda with the Maryland plates
was Mel's or not, if the lights glowing from the kitchen
window meant she was in there.

With her daughter.

You know, you tell yourself what's past is past. That
time inevitably fades reality. If not warps it into something else altogether. Then something, anything—a word,
a thought, a scent—and it all comes rushing back.

His father hadn't said much, muttering something about
how his tail was going to be in a sling as it was. Meaning,
Ryder surmised, that his mother had been behind whatever had gone down. No shocker there, given her obsessive
protectiveness of his younger brother. Who, according to
Ryder's father, had known about the baby—

Holy hell. After an hour, the shock hadn't even begun
to wear off. He pushed out a short, soundless laugh—he'd
finally gotten to the point, if barely, where he no longer

felt as though he had a rusty pitchfork lodged in his chest, and now…this.

Even if he had no idea yet what "this" was. If anything.

Frankly, if the child *had* been his—if that had even been a possibility, of course—he doubted he could have been more stunned. Or furious. Hell, Ryder couldn't decide which was eating him alive more—that Jeremy had knocked Mel up or that everybody had kept it a secret all these years. That Mel hadn't told him—

You feel betrayed? Really?

The front door opened. Ryder slouched behind the wheel like some creepy stalker, even as he silently lowered his window to get a better look, rain be damned. So, yeah, the car was Mel's—even over the deluge he could hear her still-infectious laughter before he saw her, and the memories flooded his thoughts like soldiers charging into battle. Somehow, he steeled himself against them as the kid emerged first, her tall, thin frame swallowed up in a lime-green down vest, the feeble porch light glancing off a headful of blazing curls before she yanked her sweatshirt hood up over them. She tramped to the edge of the wide porch to glare over the railing. At the weather, he guessed.

Crap. She looked exactly like Jeremy.

Ryder's heart thumped when Mel backed through the door, her translucent, bright pink plastic rain poncho making her look as though she'd been swallowed alive by a jellyfish. He couldn't tell much, other than she'd traded in those godawful Birkenstocks for even more godawful Crocs. In a bilious pink to coordinate with the poncho, no less.

Ryder felt his mouth twitch: fashion never had been her strong suit.

The door locked, Mel joined her daughter to give her a one-armed hug, laying her cheek atop her curls, and his lungs seized. Of course, between the downpour and the sketchy light from the streetlamp, he couldn't really see her face, although there was no reason why she wouldn't be as pretty as ever, her thick dark hair—still long, he saw—a breath-stealing contrast to her light, gray green eyes. Something he hadn't dared tell her then, despite how badly he knew she'd needed to hear it. Her posture, however, as she held her little girl close, her obvious sigh as her gaze drifted over what must have seemed like a bad dream, positively screamed *Just kill me now.*

It occurred to him he didn't know if she was in a relationship. Or even married. If she'd gone to college, or what she'd majored in if she had.

If she was happy, or heartbroken, or bored with her life—

No. Mel would never be bored.

He had no intention of ambushing her. Not yet, anyway. As it was, he was pressing an unfair advantage simply by being here, especially since he doubted she had any idea he knew she'd returned, let alone about Quinn. And he certainly wasn't about to confront her—not the right word, but the only one he could think of at the moment—before the million and one thoughts staggering around inside his brain shook off their drunken stupor and started talking sense. Or before he shook loose the full story from his mother—the next item on his to-do list, in fact. But for reasons as yet undefined he'd simply wanted to…see her.

The poncho glimmered in the sketchy light as Mel said something to the girl. He couldn't hear their exchange, but damned if Quinn's dramatic gestures didn't remind him exactly of her mother at that age, and it suddenly seemed incomprehensible, that he'd known absolutely nothing about the last ten years of her life when he'd been privy to pretty much all of it up to that point.

Those huge, curious eyes had hooked Ryder from the moment he saw her when she was two days old, as though—or so it seemed to his five-year-old self—she was asking him to watch out for her. Never mind that her parents lived in the groundskeeper's cottage and he in the main house, the oldest son of her parents' employers. He was hers, and she was his, and that was that, he now thought with a slight smile.

Images floated through, of her belly laugh when he'd play peekaboo with her, of helping her learn to walk, ride a tricycle, learn her alphabet. Then, later, how to throw a baseball, and cannonball into the swimming pool, and lob water balloons with deadly, and enviable, accuracy— activities his four-years-younger brother Jeremy, coddled and cosseted long after a full recovery from a severe bout of pneumonia as a toddler, found stupid and/or boring.

Of course, as Ryder grew older Mel's constantly trailing him like a duckling sometimes annoyed him no end, when he wanted to hang with his fifth-grade homies or build his model airplanes without some five-year-old *girl* yakking in his ear. A five-year-old girl with no compunction whatsoever about slugging him, hard, when he'd tell her to beat it, before stomping off, her long, twin ponytails flopping against her back.

Until he'd come to his senses—or his friends would go home—and he'd seek her out again, finding her in the kitchen "helping" her mother, Maureen, cook, or building castles out of his cast-off Legos.

And she always greeted him with a bright grin, his rejection forgiven, forgotten, Ryder thought with a pang as, shrieking the whole way, Mel and the kid finally dashed down the steps to her car.

His window raised, he watched the Honda cautiously take off through the downpour, thinking how he'd always been able to count on that grin, even after he was in high school and Mel barely up to her ankles in the first waves of adolescence, when their mothers began to cast leery glances in their direction. Although it was absurd, that they'd even think what they were thinking. Mel was his little *sister,* for God's sake, a take-no-crap punk kid who knew everything she needed to know about how boys thought…from Ryder. The boundaries couldn't have been brighter if they'd been marked in Kryptonite.

Until the summer after she turned sixteen.

He'd just finished pre-med. And oh, how grateful he'd been, after that semester from hell, for Mel's easy, no-demands company, even if the sight of her in that floral two-piece swimsuit seriously threatened those boundaries. She'd always been more mature than most girls his own age. That summer, when her body caught up to her brain…yowsa. And, yes, not being totally clueless, it was evident she no longer looked at him the same way, either.

However. He would have lopped off an appendage—in particular the one giving him five fits those days—before violating her trust. Except it had been that very trust that sent her into his arms, the day after her father's sudden death, for the comfort she couldn't get from anyone else. Especially not her wrecked mother.

Even after all this time, a wave of hot shame washed over Ryder as he remembered how desperately he'd wanted to accept what she was offering. How horrified he'd been. And he'd panicked, pure and simple. Pushed her away, walked away…*run* away, back to school weeks before he needed to be there.

She'd meant more to him than anyone else in the world, and he'd bungled things, big-time. Stomped on her already broken heart like a mad elephant. Worse, he'd never apologized, never explained, never tried to fix what he'd broken, partly because, at twenty-one, he had no clue how to do that.

But mainly because…he'd wanted her. And what kind of perv did that make him?

Groaning, Ryder let his head fall back, his own still-bruised heart throbbing inside his chest. This was the last thing he needed, to have that particularly egregious period of his life return to chomp his behind when his heart was still so sore. But chomp, it had.

He'd never expected to see Mel again, never imagined he'd have the opportunity to tell his side of the story. Not that there was any guarantee she'd even want to hear it after all this time. Nor would he blame her.

However—he finally started the car, eased down the road that led to his parents' house, on the other side of the cove—he did want to hear *Mel's* side. Which would be the side, he thought as bile rose in his throat, that explained how she'd come to have his brother's baby.

"You *told* him?" Knowing, and not caring, that she probably looked as though she'd been goosed, Lorraine Caldwell gaped at her husband as a brutal cocktail of emotions threatened to knock her right on her fanny. "Are you out of your *mind?*"

Settled into his favorite wing-chair in the wood-paneled den, the dogs dozing at his feet, David swirled his two fingers of Scotch in his glass and shrugged. Even after nearly thirty-five years of marriage, Lorraine still hadn't decided if his unflappability soothed her or unnerved her. Until she remembered they probably wouldn't still *be* married otherwise, considering…things. Things not given a voice for more than three decades, but which still occasionally shimmered between them like a ghost that refused to move on. Now, underneath blue eyes that had knocked her off her feet as a girl, a slight smirk told her that he had the upper hand. And wasn't about to let it go.

"And if you remember I was the one who said you were out of *your* mind, thinking you could keep this a secret."

David hadn't exactly been on board with the arrangement, Lorraine thought with a mix of aggravation and—dare she admit it?—admiration. Now. Then, however...

"She wasn't supposed to come back! Especially with..." She lowered her voice, despite their being alone. Even though they hadn't had full time help in years, old habits die hard. "The child. That was the agreement."

"Clearly you didn't consider all eventualities. Believe it or not, Lorraine, you can't control the entire world."

Lorraine's eyes burned. The entire world? There was a laugh. How about even her own tiny corner of it? "For heaven's sake, David—maybe they wouldn't even have run into each other. Why on earth did you jump the gun?"

"Because," he said, standing, "it didn't feel right to leave it to chance. Catching Ryder off guard if they did cross paths. Besides, aren't you even curious about her?"

Talking about being caught off guard. Lorraine sucked in a breath: she'd never, not once, indulged herself in pointless "what ifs?" After all, she'd made the best decision, the only decision, she could have made at the time. A decision circumstances had forced her to make. To change the rules now—

"What about Jeremy?" she said, grasping at rapidly disintegrating straws. "And Caroline. They've only been married six months—" At her husband's quelling look, Lorraine blew out a sigh. "What if Ryder confronts him? Did you think of that?"

"I imagine he will," David said with a shrug. "Hell, I was all for making the boy own up to his idiocy at the time—"

"Then why didn't you?" Ryder said quietly from the doorway, making Lorraine jump.

David waved his nearly empty glass in her direction. "Ask your mother."

Wordlessly, Ryder turned his gaze on her, his hands shoved into the pockets of that awful old windbreaker he'd had since college. Whereas her younger son had always been given to flying off the handle—her fault, she supposed—Ryder had always been the even-tempered one, even as a toddler. Just like his father. That had unnerved her, too, his seeming imperviousness to anything that would try to unseat him. Now, however, Lorraine could tell by the glint in his dark brown eyes, the hard set to his beard-hazed jaw—another "style" also picked up in college—that his customary calm masked an anger so intense she almost couldn't look at him.

Especially since that angry gaze relentlessly poked at the guilt she'd done her best to ignore for the past ten years.

Secrets, she thought on an inward wince. You would think she'd have learned her lesson the first time, wouldn't you?

Apparently not.

Ryder watched his mother, still attractive in an old-money, take-me-as-you-find-me way, sink into the sofa's down-filled cushions, sighing when one of the dogs heaved herself to her feet and plodded over to lay her head in his mother's lap. A pair of silver clips held her fading red curls back from her sharply boned face; in her rust-colored cardigan, jeans and flats, she gave off a certain Kate Hepburn vibe most people found intimidating. And, to a certain extent, fascinating.

Most people. Not Ryder.

"Well?" he prompted.

She distractedly traced the design of the Waterford lamp beside her before folding her hands on her lap. "The thing between Jeremy and Mel…we had no idea. None. Until Maureen marched Mel in here—into this very room, in fact—that fall and announced that Mel was pregnant." His mother shot a brief glance in his direction. "Frankly, we assumed the baby was yours." Her mouth twisted. "Until we did the math."

Too angry to speak, Ryder crossed his arms high on his chest. "And when you realized it wasn't?"

"Jeremy was barely eighteen," his mother said, her gaze fixed on the golden retriever's smooth head as she stroked it. "He'd just started at Columbia…" She pushed out a truncated sigh. "It was perfectly obvious it was all a mistake. That it meant nothing. To him, especially, but even Mel admitted…"

When Lorraine looked away, Ryder prodded, "Mel admitted what?"

"That she didn't love Jeremy. Oh, for heaven's sake, Ryder—don't look at me like that. It was a silly summer fling, nothing more. A silly summer fling with dire consequences," his mother finished on a grimace. "But then, Jeremy could hardly be blamed, could he? Not with the way M-Mel kept flaunting herself in those short shorts and tight tops—"

As in, cut-offs and T-shirts. Same as every other high school girl wore.

"And that *bathing* suit—"

"So, what? She's automatically the guilty party because she grew breasts?"

Twin dots of pink bloomed on his mother's cheeks. "Of course not. But she didn't have to be so, so *blatant* about them. She could have dressed less…enticingly. I mean, you know your brother—"

Behind them, his father huffed out a breath. "Lorraine, for pity's sake."

"Well, it's true. She played right into his hand."

"Literally," Ryder muttered, his own fisting inside his pockets. "You know, being neither blind nor gay, I was pretty aware of Mel's…assets, too. Assets she didn't flaunt any more than any other girl her age. Less, in fact, than most. That bathing suit—sure, it showed off her curves, but we're not talking a string bikini, for heaven's sake." Ryder glowered at his mother. "Yeah, I know Jeremy. But I would've thought…"

His mother stood. "You can't lay this whole thing at his feet, Ryder. Even though I know you'd love to do that. I never did understand why the two of you never got along, which is one reason we decided it was better to keep this from you. Because I knew how much it would hurt you, that Mel…" At Ryder's glare, Lorraine pressed her lips together, shaking her head.

"However, I refused to let one mistake derail Jeremy's plans. Not after he'd had to work so hard to get into Columbia. So we struck a deal—one Maureen agreed to, by the way—that in exchange for our financial support they'd leave St. Mary's for good and we'd never speak of any of this again."

As livid as he was, Ryder felt his eyes narrow. Something was off. Not so much what his mother was saying but how she was saying it. But right now he just wanted the facts.

"So it never occurred to you to make Jeremy own up to his part in this?"

"At eighteen? What on earth was he supposed to do?"

"And Mel was *six*teen. Something tells me she definitely got the short end of the stick—"

"I tried to make her see reason!" his mother said, and

he caught the flash of desperation in her eyes. "To explore her…options, but she was having none of it. She insisted on having, and keeping, the baby, although for the life of me I never understood why. That was her choice, Ryder. *Our* choice—"

"Was to let my brother off the hook by sweeping the whole thing under the rug?"

"There's a trust fund for the child. And we sent enough money through the years so they were never in any danger of starving. We honored our obligations, believe me. In the way we best saw fit. Your sister-in-law has no idea, by the way. And we'd appreciate it if you didn't tell her. It could ruin their marriage. And I'm sure you wouldn't want that on your conscience."

Ryder smirked: although the news had gobsmacked him, nothing coming out of his mother's mouth now surprised him in the least. To say Lorraine Caldwell was a control freak didn't even begin to cover it. As far back as Ryder could remember his mother had ruled the household—in her childhood home, the estate having belonged to her surgeon father, her D.C.-socialite mother, long before she'd married the gentle GP who'd stolen her heart, as lore would have it, that summer when she was nineteen. As far as Ryder could tell she'd been Daddy's spoiled little princess who'd seen no reason to change her modus operandi—as in, always getting her way—when she grew up. That she still seemed to have his father, as she'd had her own, so tightly wound around her little finger was a mystery he doubted he'd ever solve.

Except Ryder now looked to his father, seeing for the first time in David's chagrined, embarrassed expression the older man's constant acquiescence to his mother's whims for what it was—weakness, pure and simple. *For God's sake, grow a pair!* he wanted to shout, even as his heart cracked a little more, that the man he'd so wanted to believe in, look up to, apparently didn't really exist. For his dedication to his work, his patients, Ryder would always admire him. But respect him as a man? As someone he could count on to do the right thing?

Not so much.

Disheartened, he thought back to that silent promise he'd made to that chubby, bald, two-day-old baby, to look out for her. Protect her. Only he'd no idea at the time it would be his own family he'd have to protect her from. Or at the very least, try to undo ten years' worth of damage.

"No," he said to his mother. "I swear I won't breathe a word to Caroline. That's not my place, it's Jeremy's. Whose conscience, frankly, could use a good swift kick in the ass. But whatever. However, now that I know I have a niece, you better believe she's going to know at least one member of this family gives a damn about her."

"And what if Mel isn't on board with that idea?"

He looked from one to the other. "That's between Mel and me. Because you two officially have nothing more to say about it."

Chapter Two

All that food in the house, and Mel and Quinn both decided they'd rather have stir-fry. Go figure. But at least by the time they finished shopping at the only decent supermarket in town, she'd stopped looking over her shoulder, convinced Ryder—or worse, one of his parents—was going to appear at the end of every aisle. She'd driven by the clinic, seen his name beside his father's; a quick Google search on her phone revealed that Jeremy was a junior partner at some hot-shot law firm in New York.

"Hey, Virginia plates," Quinn said as Mel's headlights stabbed at the weather-and-time ravaged house, as well as the late model Lexus parked in the driveway. The rain had finally let up, although it had turned bone-chillingly cold. Welcome to early fall on the Eastern Shore. "Whose car is that?"

"I'm gonna guess April's," Mel said, all bittersweet ache at the prospect of seeing her cousin again after more than a decade. She and April had chatted briefly the day before, but only long enough to coordinate their schedules. And unleash a boatload of memories.

And laughter.

We were happy here, Mel thought on a smile, even as the backs of her sinuses twinged. *She'd* been happy here, during those summers when Amelia called enough of a truce with Mel's mother to allow Mel to hang out in the rambling old house with her close-in-age cousins. Summer sisters, they'd called themselves—

"Ohmigosh! There you are!"

In a flippy little plaid skirt and coordinating cardigan, April—still tiny and bubbly and strawberry blonde—burst out of the front door and down the steps before they'd even climbed out of the Honda, where she grabbed Mel in a hug hard enough to do damage, then let go to fan her now tear-streaked face.

"Honest to Pete," Mel said, laughing, digging in her gargantuan purse for a pack of tissues which she handed to her cousin. "Still?"

"I know, I know, I'm terrible!" Gal always had cried at the drop of a hat. "But I can't help it, it's just so good to *see* you…wait," she said, her soggy gaze turning to Quinn, standing off to one side. "Oh, my word—is that *your* little girl?"

"Little girl?" Mel said, pretending to look shocked. "What little girl? For heaven's sake, she must've crawled in the backseat while I was at the store—"

"Mo-om, geez," Quinn said. Rolling her eyes. Then she extended her hand to April. "I'm Quinn. The sane one—"

"Don't you go giving me your hand—come here, sugar," April said, hauling Quinn into her arms, and Mel's own eyes watered. Yes, April had cried more than ten girls put together, but this was what Mel remembered most about her cousin, that she *loved* more than any human being she'd ever known. That her tenderheartedness was only surpassed by an unfeigned generosity that put most people to shame.

Then she noticed how the feeble porch light glinted off the tasteful, but impressive, array of diamonds on April's ring finger. Between those and the car, Mel got the feeling her cousin was a lot better off than when they'd been kids. Not that they'd ever discussed such things, even when they were all old enough to figure out that while their grandmother obviously had money—then, at least—her three daughters had all somehow bounced well out of range of that particular tree.

"Aren't you the prettiest thing?" April now said, holding Quinn at arm's length before turning to Mel. "I take it she looks like her daddy, since I'm not seeing a whole lot of you in that face—"

"Quinn, let's get this food out of the car," Mel said, smartly going around to the trunk. "Stir-fry for dinner okay with you?"

April shot her a look, but took the hint and simply said, "Sure thing. I'm starved!"

Despite their earlier attack on the kitchen, the cloying dampness assaulted Mel's nose as they carted the groceries through the conglomeration of dusty wicker and sisal and faded pastels hunched together on scabrous floors in the large gathering room, every surface obliterated by their grandmother's "collections." Dusty paintings hung askew on walls gone cobweb-gray; mismatched shelves bowed under the weight of hundreds, if not thousands, of books and DVDs and videotapes. At least there weren't any cats.

That they'd found, at any rate.

"I had no idea the place had gone to seed like this," April whispered to Mel as they loaded the bags onto the now disinfected pine table in the middle of the oversize kitchen. Quinn dumped her bags, as well, then took off to continue exploring. Mel was half tempted suit up the kid in hazmat attire. And maybe a cross.

"Seed, hell," Mel muttered as she hauled two gallons of milk onto the top shelf of the fridge, which at least was no longer toxic. "The ancient Greeks had nothing on the civilizations growing in there."

"So you're saying it was worse?"

"Heh." April stared at one of the kitchen chairs; Mel chuckled. "Your butt might smell like Pine-sol when you get up, but you're good."

"The lawyer said Nana died virtually broke," her cousin said, sitting. "That the house…this was all that was left."

"Because she clearly spent everything she had on crap she didn't need," Mel said. "Have you been upstairs yet?"

"After seeing the gathering room? I didn't have the nerve. Not alone, anyway. And you let Quinn go up there?"

"She's an intrepid soul, she'll be fine."

April sighed. "I cannot imagine how long it's gonna take to sort through all this junk. Although I don't suppose it was junk to Nana. And who knows? There might be some valuable stuff in amongst all that…" She waved her hand, searching for the right word.

"Trash? I seriously doubt it. Frankly, my vote is for lighting a match." Mel lifted her hands. *"Oops."*

"Bite your tongue," her cousin said, coloring. "And you know she used to have good things. I remember the crystal. And the china. And some of the furniture dated back to when the house was built—"

"And sometimes, old is just old. April—the place is about to collapse, from what I can tell—"

"I'm sure most of it's cosmetic!" At Mel's snort, she added, "You mark my words, once we get it all cleared out…" Her eyes filled. "We can bring it back to life, Mel. I'm sure of it."

Too tired to argue, Mel changed the subject. "So… you're married, huh?" April frowned slightly. Readying the veggies for slaughter on a cutting board in the middle of the kitchen table, Mel pointed to her cousin's left hand with one of the knives she'd hauled from Baltimore. Because some things, a real cook doesn't leave home without.

"Oh," April said, touching the rings. "I am. Or rather, was. Clayton—my husband—died a few months ago."

"Oh, God, honey—"

"It's okay, he'd been ill for a long time." Then she squinted up at the forlorn schoolhouse-style fixture dangling in the center of the room. "That has got to go."

"And it will, when the flames reach the kitchen." Mel clanged her iron skillet onto the gas range, turned the heat on high, then returned to the table. "I take it you don't want to talk about your husband?"

"Not any more than you do the house, apparently."

"I did talk about the house, I suggested we level it and collect the insurance. That, or turn it into an annual Halloween attraction." At her cousin's silence, she frowned. "What?"

"Nothing."

"Nothing, my hiney." Mel waved the knife in April's direction. "I remember that look. All too well. That look spells trouble."

On a soft laugh, April reached across the table to briefly squeeze Mel's wrist, before grabbing a red pepper slice and nibbling on it. "It's nice, being here with you again."

"Ditto. Although…I'm not the same person I was then."

"Who is?" April said on a sigh. "Even so, despite the clutter and the filth and wildlife I don't even want to think about, being back here…it's like time stood still. Not that I feel like when we were kids—and heaven knows I wouldn't want to—but it's like the me I am now can feel the me I was then looking over my shoulder. Didn't expect that." She paused, then said, "So did you keep up with Ryder or what?" When Mel shot her a what-the-hell look, April grinned. "It's hardly an illogical question, Mel. Well?"

"No."

"Really? I mean, I know how close you two were—"

"We were childhood buddies, that's all," Mel said, wondering if it was too late to bake something. As if that was a serious question. "Besides, he went off to med school, and Mama and I moved to Baltimore after Dad died, and… we lost touch—"

Quinn bounded into the kitchen—Mel had often wondered if the child had springs on the soles of her feet—and straight to the table to snatch a carrot slice. "When's dinner? I'm about to *expire* from hunger."

"Ten minutes," Mel said, carting the chopped veggies to the stove to dump them into the sizzling oil. "You can set the table. Dishes are up there." She nodded toward the cupboard next to the sink. "Used to be, anyway."

After filching a pepper slice, Quinn swung open the cupboard door, nearly gagging when she pulled down an avocado-green Fiestaware plate that looked like it hadn't been washed in twenty years. "Gross!"

"Hey," April said with a laugh. "When we were kids we'd've rinsed it off and called it good."

"And you, child of mine," Mel said as she stirred, "used to lick the kitchen floor."

Shock and horror bloomed in Quinn's blue eyes. "Did not!"

"Got the video to prove it. You apparently have the immune system of an android. Palmolive's right on the sink, baby. Go for it."

After dinner, during which they talked, and laughed, and reminisced more than Mel had any idea they could, Quinn disappeared again to poke through those ten thousand books—heaven!—while April and Mel cleaned up. Her hands deep in Palmolive suds, April looked over at Mel, drying the dishes and stacking them on the counter rather than putting them back with their disgusting little friends.

"Dinner was fantastic. You always cook like that?"

"Thanks. And yes. Cooking's my thing."

"Really? Huh." Behind her, Mel heard sudsy swishing. "So…is Quinn's father in the picture?"

"Nope," Mel said lightly. "Never has been."

More swishing. Then: "Is she Ryder's kid?"

Yeah, she'd expected that. Still, the assumption needled. Especially since there were other people in town who'd be all too eager to leap to the same conclusion. "No. As I said, Ryder and I were friends. Good friends." She felt a tight smile tug at her mouth. "There was no way anything untoward would have happened between us. He would have never let it." At her cousin's silence, Mel turned. "What? You don't believe me?"

"Oh, I believe you. But I also remember that last summer we were all together, when Ryder took the three of us out on his dad's boat." Hauling the clean skillet onto the drainboard, April slid Mel a devilish grin. "I *also* remember the way he looked at you when he thought nobody would notice." A wet hand pressed to her chest, she released an exaggerated sigh. "And *I* thought if a boy looked at me like that? I'd absolutely die of happiness. *Die,* I tell you."

"And *how* many romance novels did you read that summer?"

April belted out a laugh, the sound unexpected from her

delicate frame. "Best. Summer. Ever," she said, and even Mel had to smile, at how they'd discovered their grandmother's stash of old, yellowing Harlequins in a trunk on the porch, clandestinely stashing them in their beach towels to read aloud to each other as they sunbathed. Damn books were probably still in the house somewhere. If they hadn't completely disintegrated by now—

"However," her cousin went on, "I also caught the way you looked at *him.* And don't you dare try to deny it. These eyes know what they saw, yes, they do."

Overhead, Mel heard the floorboards creak. "Fine," she said with a quick glance toward the ceiling. Either Quinn had changed rooms upstairs or there was a raccoon the size of Cincinnati up there. "So I might have had a little crush on him. I mean, I suppose it was inevitable, considering how kind he'd always been to me."

April laughed again. And flicked water at her.

"He was my *friend,* April," Mel said, zapping her cousin with the damp towel. "And that was the only thing that mattered."

Wringing out the sponge and laying it on the edge of the sink, April turned to her with a frown. "Then why'd you two stop talking to each other?"

"Because we just did!" Mel slammed the last plate a little too hard on the pile, then shut her eyes, thinking, *Yeah, hand her the gun to shoot you with, why not?*

She heard April dump the sudsy water into the sink, yank another dishtowel off the old "finger" rack under the counter.

"That's probably not dry yet," Mel muttered. "I just washed it this afternoon."

"It's fine." April wiped her hands and hung the towel back up, then leaned closer to the sink to look out the window at the plum-colored sky. "I didn't mean to upset you, honey. But being back here…guess it's made me a little melancholy. Like I want to recapture a little of that magic, you know?"

"I do, actually. But it's not possible."

"I know. Still, it's sad. You and Ryder losing touch." She turned to Mel. "Don't you think?"

"I don't. Think about it, I mean." Or at least she hadn't until a five-minute phone call once more snatched the rug right out from under her.

"You think you'll see him while you're here?"

"Not planning on it. And can we *please* change the subject—?"

The doorbell rang. After a fashion. "Oh! I bet that's Blythe," April said, heading out of the kitchen. "Last time we talked she said she didn't know if she'd get in tonight or tomorrow…"

Not at all sure if she was ready to deal with her older, bossier cousin, Mel turned on the old radio that had been in that same spot on the counter forever, fiddling with the dial until she picked up some oldies rock station from Dover…the same music her mother had listened to while cooking in the Caldwells' kitchen when she'd been growing up. Over Simon and Garfunkel's "The Sound of Silence"—heh—she heard April's cheery, non-stop prattle coming closer. Steeling herself, Mel turned, a forced smile stretching her cheeks.

And nearly passed out.

"That last thing you were saying? You might want to revise that," April said, clearly enjoying the heck out of the moment before she vanished, leaving Mel to face Ryder all by her little self.

Ridiculously handsome, all-grown-up, obviously angry-as-hell Ryder.

Yippee-skippy.

* * *

"How'd you know I was here?"

Mel had left Quinn with her cousin—since no way was she going to have this little reunion in her daughter's presence—but it'd taken her a good ten minutes to work up to the question. This being the awkward moment from hell and all. Now she sensed Ryder—who hadn't exactly been chatty, either—glance over as they strolled, bundled up against the frigid night air, along the marina at the edge of town. A trek they'd made innumerable times as kids, at all times of the day and night, in every imaginable kind of weather. Mostly just for something to do away from the adults, sometimes on their bikes or inline skates when there weren't too many people around....

And cocooning herself in the used-to-bes wasn't going to do a blessed thing to stop the vague nausea brought on by having to face the right-nows.

"Phil Paxton told my dad," Ryder said, that comfortingly familiar voice conjuring up so much of what she'd made herself forget, and there it was, the past colliding with her present, boom. Even his obvious irritation provoked memories, of when he'd get ticked off over some dumb prank or other she'd pulled as a kid. Man, this was doing even stranger things to her head than walking back into her grandmother's house. "Said Amelia'd left you three her place, that you were coming down to get everything in order."

"Big mouth," she muttered.

"Was it supposed to be a secret?"

At the word "secret," Mel flinched, then dug a tissue out of the down vest she'd thrown over her hoodie to wipe her drippy nose. "I don't suppose."

"Anything else you'd like to share?"

No need to ask what he meant, since the disbelief icing

his words said it all. Even so, she had no idea what she was and wasn't allowed to say, to admit to, even now. "Depends. What've you heard?"

"That you and Jeremy had a kid together."

She stuffed the tissue back in her pocket. "Jeremy may be Quinn's biological father, but to say we had her *together* is a stretch."

Silence crackled between them, far more biting than the damp air, until Ryder finally broke it with, "God, Mel— *why?*"

"Because I was a mess and he was there." *And you weren't,* she thought, startled at the residual anger after all this time. "Sad, but true." More silence, punctuated by the soft clattering of the docked boats, Ryder's steady footsteps against the wood. "When did you find out?"

"Late this afternoon."

"I don't mean that I was coming down—"

"Not talking about that."

"You really had no idea?"

"Nope."

"Wow," she said on a strangled half laugh, her breath misting around her face. "I can't believe they actually took it that far. I assumed you knew."

Ryder raised his arms to flip the collar of his jacket up around his neck. "Because I never contacted you again?"

"Yeah."

He shook his head, then thrust his hands into his pockets. "That wasn't the reason."

When no further explanation seemed to be forthcoming, Mel wandered out underneath the gazebo-like structure at the end of the marina to fold her arms across the top railing, deeply inhaling the tangy, bone-chilling breeze. Moonlight flicked at the black, rippling water below. Pretty. When Ryder mimicked her pose, the wind ruffling his short, dark hair, she said, "I can't even imagine how ticked you must be right now."

"No. You can't." He glanced at her. "My folks said Jeremy knows."

"He always has."

"And he's never—?"

"Nope. Far as he's concerned Quinn never happened."

He leaned harder on the railing to press his head into his palms, then dropped them again. "Does she ask? About her father?"

"Until recently? Not as much as you might think. Although…" Mel forced air into her lungs, annoyed that she still felt like she was breathing through broken glass. "I was seriously involved with someone for two years. Thought…this was it. *He* was it. Quinn became very attached. Enough that she didn't ask about her daddy because she'd assumed she'd found one."

"This isn't going to end well, is it?"

And there it was, despite everything, that same kindness and understanding that had seen her through her entire childhood, that made her eyes sting even now. "His ex popped back into his life. And right into the bastard's bed, apparently. Turns out he'd never really gotten over her. Our virtually living in each other's pockets notwithstanding. Although…" She twisted to lean one elbow on the railing, looking at Ryder. "He did offer to make me a partner. In his restaurant," she added at Ryder's quick frown.

"After…?"

"Oh, as in, right on the heels of. Consolation prize, yay," she said, then hmmphed. "Guess he figured that was the least he could do. Considering it was my mad cooking skills that'd made the place as successful as it was."

A hint of a smile played across Ryder's mouth. "And you walked."

"As fast as these cute little feet could carry me."

"Good for you."

"In theory, sure. In practical terms, not so much. Oh, I've managed, working for caterers off and on, but nothing's come along that even begins to compare. I really, really loved that job. Made me stretch as a chef, try new things. And the partnership would've been an incredible opportunity. If I'd had a heart made of stone."

"How long ago was this?"

"A few months," she said, even though the date was indelibly, and regrettably, forever etched in her brain. "Dammit, Ry—I never saw it coming. Neither did Quinn. And it was especially hard on her since my mother died last year. She and Quinn were extremely close, as you can imagine."

"Damn, honey. I'm sorry."

Mel nodded, then said, "Quinn's just now getting over it, I think. Hope. The breakup, I mean. She doesn't mention it, in any case."

"And you?" he said gently.

"I alternate between numb and mad-as-hell. Although I'm at least through the eating anything that isn't nailed down stage." She sighed. "But now that we're once again in daddyless mode, yeah, Quinn's started asking about her father. Not a subject I'm wild about discussing when I'm *not* wishing bad things on half the human population. Best I could come up with was telling her he vanished before she was born, he didn't know she was coming, that I have no idea where he is. How to find him."

"You lied?"

She snorted a humorless laugh. "How do you tell a child her father really didn't want her? That his parents paid me off to never contact him, or show my face in St. Mary's, ever again? And how in *God's* name…" She swallowed. "How do I explain that her mother was every bit as complicit in this little scheme as the people who've been paying her hush money since before she was born?"

"Mel, for God's sake—you were sixteen."

"Seventeen, by the time she arrived. But yeah. Even so, I can't pretend I didn't know what I was doing. That I'd more or less sold my soul—or at least, my integrity—in order to provide for my child. And it's eating me up, living this lie."

Expelling a harsh sigh, Ryder grasped the railing, not looking at her. "Not any more than it's eating *me* up, that when you get right down to it, this is all my fault."

"And how on earth do you figure that?"

"So you didn't hook up with Jeremy to get back at me?"

It was funny, really, if you thought about it: years of experience had taught Mel that few human males seemed ready, or able, to accept responsibility for anything. At least, the human males *in* her experience. To the point where she'd forgotten that Ryder had probably been the most responsible human being she'd ever met. Except, because Ryder *had* been stalwart and noble and honorable as all hell, in a convoluted way he had a point.

"Didn't say that," she said at last. "But it's ridiculous to blame you for my actions. No matter what I might have told myself at the time." She paused, then breathed out, "Please don't hate me, Ryder. Since I still hate myself plenty enough for both of us."

Ryder's chest constricted at the self-deprecation trying so damn hard to undermine Mel's tough bunny persona. He looked away, giving her the space she clearly wanted. And he needed. Because he had no idea how to bind up her wounds when his own were still so fresh.

Even as the old compulsion reared its head, refusing to be ignored.

"How could I possibly hate you when I'm the one who botched things so badly—"

"What you did was save me from making an idiot of myself." Her mouth twisted. "At least, that night."

Acid flared in his gut. "Still. I could've handled the situation with a bit more…grace. And afterwards…I should have called. Emailed, something. To check on you, make sure you were okay. I mean, I owed you that much."

"Owed me?" Mel gave him a puzzled look. "You didn't—don't—owe me anything—"

"You were *grieving,* Mel. Whatever else might have been going on, you came to me for comfort, and instead of figuring out how to give you what you really needed I pushed you away. Harshly, if memory serves. So you can't possibly be beating yourself up more than I am. On that score, I figure we're probably about even—"

Her sharp laugh caught him up short. "Did you really think my actions that night were solely motivated by grief? Yeah, that might've short-circuited my inhibitors, but I wanted you because I wanted you." She looked away. "Because I was sick to death of being treated like a little sister. Stupid, huh?"

Ryder looked up into the navy sky before saying, very quietly, "Then you have no idea how much of a struggle it was to turn you down."

He felt her eyes on the side of his face for several beats before a soft, startled laugh fell out of her mouth. "Holy crap. Are you *serious?*"

"Yep. And you can stop laughing," he said, even as chagrin pushed at the corners of his own mouth. Then he sighed. "All our lives, I thought of myself as your protector. A role I took very seriously—"

"Tell me about it."

"—and you were a kid. Legally, anyway. And what I'd

begun to feel for you…inappropriate doesn't even begin to cover it. No way on God's earth was I going to act on what I was feeling, but damn, it scared me. That everything our relationship was predicated on…" He scrubbed the heel of his hand across his jaw, then banged it against the railing. "What you wanted that night—hell, what *I* wanted—redefined *wrong*. You'd always trusted me. And I refused to violate that trust. Even though it nearly killed me."

She took a deep breath. "So you freaked."

"To put it mildly. No matter what I did, I was going to hurt you. Worse than you already were. And afterward, when I went back to school…" His gaze touched hers. "I had no idea how to fix it."

Yanking her sweatshirt hood up over her head, Mel faced the moonlight-stippled currents for some time before finally saying, "It took a while, but eventually I got over the rejection. Once the hormone fog cleared. Because, like you said, what else could you have done? Your silence, though… That devastated me, Ry. Not gonna lie."

His gut twisted. "So you got even."

"Not on purpose," she said after a moment. "I mean, I didn't set my sights on your brother. Small consolation though that might be."

Ryder frowned. "He came on to you?"

"Not blatantly, no. Not at first, anyway. He just suddenly seemed, I don't know. Interested. Like he cared. And I was hurt, Ryder. Hurt, and confused, and adrift…" One side of her mouth ticked up. "And, okay, mad. At you, for basically walking out of my life. At myself, for being an idiot. For ruining the one good thing in it."

She paused. "I made a terrible mistake, Ryder. Not that I don't love Quinn with every fiber of my being, but the rest of it?" Her head wagged. "I disappointed everyone, especially my mother. Who adored Quinn, don't get me wrong, but I know she never quite got over how badly everything ended. Then there was Nana, who never spoke to me again—"

"This being the same woman who cut herself off from her own daughter, right? For reasons known only to herself? You're not responsible for other people's grudges, Mel. And as far as that *agreement* goes—legally it's worth bupkiss."

"Yeah, well, it's amazing, how strong a motivator fear is. You want to talk freaked?" She pointed to herself. "Poster child. And if I'm being completely honest, at least it got me out of St. Mary's. Me, and my mother, even if she never quite saw it that way. Got both of us away from…everything."

"Meaning my family."

Several beats passed before she said, "In all fairness it's not as if they treated my parents badly—and I always did have a soft spot for your father. At heart he's a good man. In fact, I gathered he was behind the generous financial considerations. And as far as Jeremy and I went—we used each other," she said flatly. "And we both knew it. So there was never any *ohmigod, you can't separate us we're in loooove* thing going on. If the dude couldn't be bothered to acknowledge his own kid, I could live with that. I hated him for it, but I could live with it. For your parents, though, to turn their backs on their first grandchild…" She gave her head a sharp shake. "For your mother to go so far as to demand that I *take care* of the 'problem'—that was a lot harder to handle."

Of course it was. Because while he may have detected a glimmer of regret in his mother's eyes, he doubted it was any match for the stubborn pride that motivated every action and decision Lorraine Caldwell had ever made. And hearing Mel echo his mother's earlier admission…

Ryder shut his eyes, wrestling to control his breathing before saying, "I want to make things up to you."

"Forget it, Ry. What's done is done."

"Even if I say I'd like to get to know Quinn? Why not?" he said when her gaze slammed into his. "Just because my brother had his head up his ass—"

Mel pushed herself away from the railing and started back down the boardwalk. "Not gonna happen."

"She's still my niece."

"Which I can't tell her, brainiac."

"They can't legally—"

"*Legal* has nothing to do with it!" she said, stopping short, the wind whipping strands of hair that had escaped the hood across her face. "I know what my rights are, okay? I know what I could do. I also know what I can't do. And *won't* do. And that's anything that could potentially hurt my kid—"

"So you're tarring me with the same brush? When I knew nothing about it?"

"You weren't there, Ryder!" she said, tears shining in her eyes. "Weren't there when your mother called me a little tramp in front of my humilated mother, who'd been loyal as hell to yours for more than twenty years! Weren't there when she accused me of trying to worm my way into the family, saying that since clearly my plan to snag you hadn't worked, I'd gone after Jeremy, or when she made me do a DNA test before Quinn was born to verify that Jeremy was really the father!"

Ryder's stomach plummeted. "Dammit—I had no idea—"

"No, you didn't. Don't. So believe me, I want less to do with your parents than they want to do with me. And if you get involved with Quinn…" She jerked away. "It won't work, Ryder. Because the past…it doesn't go *poof* simply because you want it to. But here's the weird thing…"

Suddenly calmer, as though the storm had blown over, she started walking again. "Now that I'm a mother, too? In a way I get where your mother was coming from. About how you do anything to protect your kid. I didn't—don't—agree with her methods, but I understand her motivation."

Mel's mouth pulled flat, exactly the way she used to as a child, when she'd made up her mind, by golly, and nothing and no one was going to change it. "Quinn's already hurting, from her grandmother's death, from my breakup. At least one of those things I had some control over, and I blew it. Forgot, when I went and hitched my wagon to a rainbow, there was someone else involved. So you better believe I learned my lesson. Meaning I'd hack off a limb before I'd let Quinn anywhere near the people who wrote *her* off."

Even in the dark, the pain in her eyes, her voice…

"And you thought I'd written you off, too." When she shrugged, he said, over the guilt dammed up at the back of his throat, "I swear, things would've been different if I'd known."

"Right. What on earth would you have done?"

"I don't know. Something. Married you, if nothing else—"

"Oh, yeah," Mel said on a high-pitched laugh, "your parents would've been totally on board with that idea. Do you really think they would have let you jeopardize *your* education, *your* career, when they wouldn't let Jeremy jeopardize his? And Quinn wasn't even yours! Not to mention, what makes you think I would have let you do that?"

"You can honestly say you wouldn't have even considered it? Especially given—"

"That I had the mother of all crushes on you?"

"A crush I had a damn hard time not reciprocating!"

She blinked, then released another laugh, this one softer. Sadder. "And marriage would've made it all okay? Au contraire, my friend. It would've ruined everything."

"Except I did that anyway, didn't I?"

On a cross between a groan and a growl, Mel clamped her hands to her head, tromping down off the boardwalk to the parking lot. "God, why are we even talking about this? Like we can somehow change what happened? It's done, it's over, and the second this business with Nana's house is straightened out, I'm outta here. So you tell your mother she has absolutely nothing to worry about, the last thing I want to do is make waves."

Nearly to the car, Ryder grabbed Mel's hand. If she was shocked, she didn't let on. Instead she calmly met his gaze, her brows slightly raised.

"I know I can't even begin to fix what my family broke. Or even what I broke. But to at least honor what we had—"

"What we had doesn't exist anymore," Mel said softly, reclaiming her hand. "And it hasn't for a long, long time. We're not those two kids anymore, Ry." She smirked. "Can't go back, no way to go forward. So. Think this is what they call a non-starter—"

At the sound of some ridiculous ringtone, she dug her phone out of her pocket. "Huh. It's April…" She put the phone to her ear. "Yeah?" Ryder saw her brows crash, then she yanked open the car door. "We'll be right there."

"Everything okay?" he asked after getting in beside her, barely getting his seat belt fastened before she zoomed out of the sandy, unpaved lot and back onto the street.

"I didn't quite get it all, April wasn't making total sense, but apparently Quinn sliced her hand open on a nail or something." At Ryder's silence, she let out a sigh. "I suppose logically I should let you take a look, huh?"

"Up to you. But the nearest E.R.'s a good half hour away. And I have my bag in my car."

"Of course you do," she muttered as they flew into the weed-cracked driveway and she cut the engine. But before he could get out, she snagged his wrist. "Not one word—"

"Can I at least tell her we were friends? She's going to wonder why we were together," he said when she opened her mouth to protest. "She knows you lived here before, right? So we happened to run into each other—"

"Fine, fine, whatever." She shooed him toward the door. "Just get in there before my kid bleeds to death."

Ryder slammed shut the car door and trudged up the porch steps behind Mel, thinking he'd never been so angry, at so many people, for so many reasons, in his life.

With his own sorry hide easily taking first place.

Chapter Three

Mel was grateful to see that her cousin—who as a teen-ager would scream like a banshee if she nicked herself shaving—had either overcome her heebie-jeebies at the sight of blood or was doing a damn good job of hiding it from Quinn, seated on the counter and looking a little woozy herself. April had hidden the boo-boo, as well, wrapping it tightly in a paper towel and holding Quinn's arm up over her head.

"Oh, sweetie…" Mel rushed to her blood-smeared daughter—yeah, that top was history—forking her fingers through Quinn's curls as April, bless her heart, beat a hasty retreat. "What happened?"

"There's a dumb nail sticking out of the back door, I didn't see it," Quinn mumbled, then squinted at Ryder, who'd plunked his coat and bag on the kitchen table and was now rooting around inside it. "Who're you?"

"An old friend of your mother's," Ryder said with a

kind—and yet, still killer, go figure—smile for the kid as he carted a bottle of antiseptic and assorted packets over to lay beside Quinn on the counter. One hand propped on the edge of the worn laminate, he hooked the other on his hip. "I'm also a doctor. Convenient, huh?"

Quinn shrugged. "I guess."

On a soft chuckle, Ryder washed his hands and dried them on a paper towel, then ripped open a package of latex gloves, snapped them on. "Mind if I take a peek?"

"April said to keep my hand up 'cause of the bleeding."

"Lots of blood, huh?"

"Like you would *not* believe."

"Then April did good. But I think it's okay to lower it now." When she did, he carefully removed the blood-soaked towel. Aiyiyi. Mel told herself it would be very uncool to throw up, even if the sink was right there. "It seems to have pretty much stopped now, so that's good. You'll be back to playing the violin in no time."

Quinn giggled. "I don't play the violin, I play the piano."

"You don't say?" Another smile. "You any good?"

Not nearly as good as you are, Mel thought ruefully as her daughter's shoulders bumped. "Not really. But I've only been taking lessons for a year."

"Yeah. I took 'em for ten. Loved every minute of it."

"Really?"

"No," he said, and Quinn laughed again, and Ryder's smile melted Mel's heart, dammit to hell. Especially when he turned it on her and all—well, most—of her man-hating crazies scurried away, whimpering. "I assume her tetanus is up to date?"

"Not sure. She might be due for a booster?"

"We can take care of that, too. Okay, honey, I want you to hold your hand over the sink, I'm going to pour a bunch of this antiseptic over the wound to clean it. It's probably going to sting, but it won't last long. You ready?"

Quinn sucked in a deep breath, then nodded and gingerly stuck out her hand, wincing as Ryder cleaned it. "Almost done, you're doing great…there. Now I can see what's going on."

As he carefully inspected the gash, Quinn actually leaned closer to get a better look. As opposed to Mel, who was perfectly happy to let someone else tend to this side of things, thank you. Especially if that person was the same one who'd always been the one to patch up her various scrapes and cuts and owies when they were kids. That inline skating thing? Hadn't exactly been a natural talent—

"I'm gonna need stitches, huh?" Quinn asked, sounding more curious than worried.

"Oh, I'd say at least a hundred," Ryder said, deadpan, and Quinn giggled, and Ryder lifted his eyes—all sweetly crinkled at the corners, of course—to the little girl, and Mel saw in those eyes…too much. That while she didn't doubt that Ryder was every bit as kind and funny with all his younger patients, it was patently obvious Quinn had already grabbed his heart.

And, judging from the grin on her daughter's face, the feeling was mutual.

Ah, doom. You again, is it?

Then Ryder turned his gaze to Mel, all business, except not, and now that the urge to barf had passed she noticed a dullness in those dark eyes she hadn't noticed before, and it occurred to her how one-sided their catch-me-up conversation had been. That she had no idea what was, or had been, going on in his life. Was he married? Divorced? No ring, but that didn't mean anything—

"Actually," he said, "if the cut hadn't been where she's likely to pull it apart in normal use, I'd say we'd be good with a butterfly bandage. But to be on the safe side I think a couple of stitches are in order. Piece of cake," he said with a wink for Quinn, and Mel thought, *If only, buddy boy.*

If only.

If only, Ryder thought, removing his gloves a few minutes later after stitching up his niece's wound, one could stitch back together the ragged edges of one's life, and heart, so easily. If all it took to repair the damage was training and skill and patience. A strong stomach wouldn't hurt, either.

The booster shot administered and the wound dressed, Quinn skipped off to watch the monster, old-school TV in the gathering room—after giving Ryder a hug that scraped his still-tender heart. His eyes fixed on the kitchen doorway, he asked, "Is she always that affectionate?"

"It depends." She paused. "On whether she feels she can trust someone or not. Guess you passed."

He lowered his gaze to hers, just long enough to make her blush, then walked over to the offending nail. "Then I'm honored. She's a fun kid." He opened the door, the chilly damp barely registering in the drafty old house. Now why the heck would somebody hammer through the panel from the outside? "You got something I can pound this sucker out with?"

"Probably." Watching Mel as she began yanking open, then ramming shut, assorted swollen drawers, guilt shuddered through Ryder that he was even noticing how the soft jersey of her hoodie, the even softer fabric of her worn jeans, hugged curves that had very nicely matured—

"Sorry about the house," she said, still rummaging.

"Why? Since I assume—" he scanned the mountains of detritus "—you didn't make the mess."

"True. Still. Oh, looky…" Amidst much clattering, she

hauled a decrepit-looking hammer from one of the drawers, her brows drawn as she inspected it. "Although Noah probably used this to build the ark."

Ryder extended his hand. "If it worked for Noah, I'm good." Two whacks and the nasty thing was history, safely disposed of in the trash where it no longer posed a danger. "Next question—why isn't the heat on?"

"The thermostat's not working—"

"Where is it?"

"In the dining room, but—"

"Be right back."

A few minutes later he returned triumphant, loving Mel's dumbfounded expression when the radiators started to clank. "How'd you do that?'"

"Thermostat's fine," he said, opening cupboard doors until he found a half dozen flowery, albeit dusty, tin containers which still held an assortment of teas. "Boiler pilot light had gone out. All fixed now." He hadn't been in the house much when they were kids, and then only after Amelia had deemed her granddaughters old enough to be left on their own, but he remembered these. And, in the first one he opened, he hit pay dirt—a stash of Earl Grey. He dug out two bags and held them up. "Kettle?"

Mel frowned. "And I'm guessing those would be Mrs. Noah's tea bags."

"Eh, the boiling water will kill whatever needs killing." He waggled them, and Mel sighed. But she dragged the kettle off the stove, rinsed it out five times, then filled it and set it on the burner. "You actually went down into the basement?"

"I did. It's even scarier than it was when we were kids."

Mel sighed, then angled her head at him. "Why are you still here?"

Because the thought of going back to that empty house makes me crazy. Crazier.

"Because I'm cold as hell. And you'd hardly begrudge the man who just saved your daughter's life a cup of tea, would you?"

"Hey," April said from the doorway, wrapping a scarf around her neck. "Since the heat's on—" Mel pointed to Ryder, who waved "—the kid and I are gonna make an ice cream run. Any requests?"

"Chocolate chip," Ryder said smoothly, earning him a "Got it," from April and a glare from Mel.

"Thought you were freezing?" she said after they heard the front door close.

"I won't be by the time they get back. Especially since—" he leaned back in the chair, his arms folded high on his chest "—the heat's back on. You might want to close off the radiators in the unused rooms, though. To save fuel."

"Gah. Were you always this much of a pain in the butt?"

"No more than you were."

"Touché."   "

Okay, so it felt good, sitting here, giving her grief, letting her give him grief right back. Simply enjoying the company, he mused as he surveyed the woebegone—to the point of creepy—room. "Place needs a lot of work, doesn't it?"

"That would be our take on it, yep," Mel muttered, apparently fascinated with the flames licking at the kettle's bottom.

"Might be hard to find many buyers interested in it in this condition."

"Only need one," she said. Still watching that kettle. "And what's it to you?"

"Nothing. Nothing at all. Just making conversation."

Which sputtered and gasped for several seconds until she said, "Thank you." Her eyes touched his before veering back to the kettle. "For saving Quinn's life and all."

"Oh, that. Anytime. Although I do want to see her in a day or so, make sure everything's healing up okay."

"We can do that." The kettle whistled; seconds later she handed him a mug of steaming water. "Not sure there's any sugar—"

"This is fine," he said, dunking his tea bag. "For God's sake, Mel...sit. Talk."

She stood, her arms crossed, her mouth set. "About what?"

"The Orioles' chances at taking the Series this year, I don't know. No, wait, I've got an idea—how about you tell me all about Quinn?"

He saw her eyes fill. "Ryder—"

"Why *did* you decide to keep her?" he asked as gently as he knew how. "We get our share of teen moms at the clinic, I know how hard it is—"

"Do you?"

"Enough," he said, refusing to cow. "So, why?" He paused. "Especially considering the circumstances."

That got a tight little smile. "Hardest decision I ever had to make. Or probably ever will. But in the end I guess I just wanted her to know at least *one* of us thought she was worth keeping. Which I suppose sounds silly and romantic and totally impractical, and to be honest I don't know how I would have managed without my mother to help out, but there it is. She's mine and I'm hers and that's that."

Ryder smiled. "She's nothing like Jeremy, is she?"

After a long moment, she shook her head. "She's an awful lot like her mother, though."

"As in, silly and romantic and totally impractical?"

"Or we could go with headstrong, ruthlessly honest

and never knows when to shut up." At Ryder's laugh, Mel seemed to weigh her options for a moment before slowly lowering herself into the chair across from him, her eyes alight. "She is *so* smart, Ryder. Taught herself to read at four, she goes through library books like candy. I home-school her, so she can go at her own pace. She's reading at high school level, just finished eighth grade math. And she adores science—far more than I ever did, that's for sure."

"Wow."

"You said it. Except I don't know how much longer I can keep up with her. And now that she's so far ahead of other kids her age, putting her in public school seems pointless."

"What about a private school with a program that would challenge her?" When she got up to face the sink and the blackness outside, he took a scalding swallow of the tea, then carefully set down the mug. "There are scholarships—"

"I know. And I actually checked out a couple of schools in Baltimore, but..."

"But, what?"

She blew a short laugh through her nose, then turned back to him. "Despite our friendship, Ry, I was always extremely aware growing up that you were breaking 'the rules.' That I was the hired help's kid. And I pretty quickly figured out that people...well, we pigeonhole each other, don't we?"

"I don't," Ryder said evenly, his fingers strangling the mug's handle.

"Of course you do," she said on a sigh. "It's what human beings do. Even when we were kids, you knew you were breaking the rules, too, and don't tell me you didn't." When he glowered at the mug, she let out another little laugh. "It wasn't possible to be in the position I was in at that house and not feel 'less than.' A point more than driven home to me at the end. And I don't want Quinn to ever feel like that, as though someone was doing her a favor by 'letting' her go to a school with the rich kids."

His forehead pinched, Ryder lifted his eyes to hers. "It's not the same thing. True, my mother can be a snob, but—"

"You don't think I didn't hear your private school buddies give you grief about me? That I didn't know the real reason behind why you pushed me away when they came over? As long as our friendship stayed in the closet we were fine—"

"For heaven's sake—you were five years younger than I was! No bunch of twelve-year-old boys on earth is going to be okay with a seven-year-old hanging around with them!"

"And that's all it was?"

"Yes! Mel…where is this coming from?"

She bunched her mouth for a moment, then said, "One of your friends, I don't remember his name, brought his little sister with him a couple of times. I caught a glimpse of her from the hall when they arrived, she looked to be about my age—"

"That would've been Robbie Banes's sister. Sylvia or Sarah or something."

Mel nodded. "She saw me, too, even asked her mother if she could play with 'the little girl.' Your mother glanced in my direction, then mumbled something that sounded like 'That wouldn't be a good idea,' before steering them away."

"Oh, God…" Ryder scrubbed a hand through his hair. "Again, no idea. Although, if I'm remembering correctly we all would have been thrilled if the kid had been able to play with you. Man, what a little pill." He lifted the mug toward her. "Count yourself lucky you were spared."

"That's not the issue," she said, and he sighed.

"I know it's not. And maybe, if I'm being totally honest, there's more truth to what you were picking up on than I want to admit. Not that I didn't think my mother was full of it, but I guess I did try as much as possible to avoid rubbing her face in our friendship."

Her lips twitched in an approximation of a smile. "Thank you. For not giving me some BS."

"I would never do that. Not consciously, in any case. But believe me, our friendship was as real as it gets. Real enough to piss my mother off," he said, feeling one side of his mouth hitch.

"Which would prove my point, yes?"

"That my mother's a throwback to another era? Not going to deny it. That she speaks for her entire socio-economic class? I sure as hell hope not. And you are not going to like this, but it's not right to put your issues on Quinn."

"I'm her mother, I'll pile on whatever issues I damn well like. At least until she tells me to butt out, she can make her own decisions. Which I realize could be next week, at the rate she's going. Not a bridge I'm anxious to cross, but whatever. And she has friends, before you ask. I'm not raising her in a vacuum. We're part of a homeschooling support group, in fact. Just regular folks, happily owning our little middle-class lives—"

"And what if Quinn goes on to an Ivy League school? She's not going to live in that middle-class bubble forever."

"True. But by then she'll be old enough to handle it."

"To not be contaminated, you mean."

"Yes, I suppose." She shrugged. "It's a lot easier to pretend class differences don't exist when you're at the top of the food chain."

"Mel, this isn't making any sense. If for no other reason than your grandparents…this house…"

"Belonged to my grandfather's family. I didn't know this until a few years ago, but it seems Nana had been a store clerk or something when they married, well after his

parents' deaths. But unfortunately, at least in her genera-
tion—and in this town—marriage wasn't some alchemic
process by which a person's roots could be magically al-
tered. An Irish peasant will always be an Irish peasant. So
when my mother married your parents' groundskeeper…"

"Your grandmother had a cow."

"Try a whole herd. As though she saw my mother's decision as setting *her* back several generations, that her attempts to shake off her background had been for naught.
That Mom and Dad's marriage was a happy one meant
nothing." She blew out a sigh. "I just wonder," she said,
more to herself than to him, "why people take everything
so personally? Why we can't simply be happy for our kids
without worrying about how their actions reflect on us?"

And Ryder found himself wishing he could somehow
relieve her of at least some of the baggage crushing what
had once been the brightest spirit he'd ever known, even
if anger, crouched in the shadows of his mind, flashed
razor-edged teeth at her stubbornness, her insistence about
things he knew weren't entirely true. That they'd been so
close in many ways, and yet seen things through entirely
different lenses…not a damn thing he could do about that.

Or was there?

He got up, repacked his bag, slipped his coat back on.

"You're leaving?"

"For now."

"No ice cream?"

"Think I'll take a rain check."

She followed him through the cluttered gathering room,
like a thrift store run amok, to the front door. Once there,
Ryder suggested they exchange cell phone numbers, after
which Mel asked, "How much do I owe you? For the house
call?"

"I'll pretend I didn't hear that."

"I don't want—"

"Fine. Then…dinner. How's that?"

"And I'll pretend I didn't hear *that*."

"This isn't about Quinn."

Her chin came up. "Damn straight it isn't," she said, and he thought, *There's my girl.*

"Mel…I'm not about to out Quinn. Granted, I hate this whole secrecy thing, and I know it's going to come back and bite everyone in the butt, but I also realize how delicate the situation is. For Quinn especially. So I promise you, she will not hear the truth from me. But you might want to hold on to that sigh of relief for a second, because I'm not done."

At her wide eyes, Ryder leaned one wrist against the door jamb, leaning close enough to see Mel's pupils dilate. "But you and I were friends, and you are back, and it's high time we opened *those* closet doors, don't you think? So. Dinner," Ryder repeated. "Just you and me. In the most public venue I can think of."

"And if I say no?"

"I'm not above kidnapping you."

Her mouth twitched. "Your mother would have kittens."

"Here's hoping," he said, and she actually laughed before slowly shaking her head.

"I don't know, Ry. Could I at least think about it?"

"Of course."

And that should have been his cue to haul his sorry ass through the door and out to his car. If he'd been inclined, that is, to listen to his head and not whatever made him instead lift one hand to brush his thumb across her rapidly cooling cheek, a move that sent his stomach into a free fall, that he hadn't touched anyone like that since Deanna. Hadn't wanted to. And his wanting to now confused the hell out of him.

Mel sucked in a breath, her eyes going even bigger. "What the *hell* are you doing?"

"Seriously thinking about things I've got no right to think about," he said, realizing how hard he was frowning. That Mel's pulse had kicked up at the base of her throat. He let his hand drop, and Mel released a shaky breath.

"Ryder—"

"I'm no more interested in trying to recapture the past than you are," he said with a short, point-to-you nod. "But just to set the record straight? I didn't hurt you back then because I was rich. I hurt you because I was stupid. We clear on that?"

"Sure," she said after a moment, the single word squeezed out as though she didn't dare say anything more, and Ryder finally made his feet carry him down the porch steps.

And away from madness.

Chapter Four

Quinn had thought it was kinda weird that Ryder was already gone when she and April got back from the store, since he'd *asked* for the chocolate chip ice cream. But then, considering how weird things already were? She didn't suppose she should be surprised.

Especially with her mom. At first Quinn had been focusing too hard on her cut hand to really notice, but once Ryder got her fixed up Quinn saw that Mom was sort of rattled. And not because of Quinn's hand, which wasn't nearly as bad as when she'd been a little kid and the window in their apartment had slammed shut on her fingers, breaking two of them. *That* sucked. This was messy and all—she hadn't been kidding about the blood—but nothing to get scared about, really. But Mom had looked like she was gonna throw up. So what could it be except Ryder? Except if they'd been friends and stuff…?

It made no sense. But then, the older Quinn got, the

less anything about grown-ups made sense. They were just weird.

And she really needed to come up with a new word before she wore that one out.

So last night Mom let her eat a boatload of ice cream, and then she and April and Mom watched some dumb old movie—only it was a tape or something you had to rewind when it was finished? Weird—and then the grown-ups made her go to bed way before she was ready while they stayed downstairs and talked. Only Quinn couldn't sleep, because she kept thinking about how Mom looked like Quinn had felt when they'd gone to that fake haunted house last Halloween—even though she *knew* it was fake, she was still all nervous from thinking something was going to jump out and scare her any second.

Except it wasn't Halloween and as far as Quinn knew her great-grandmother's house wasn't haunted, pretend or otherwise. Gross and dirty and disgusting, but not haunted.

At least today was sunny and warmer and Mom had said, yeah, they could go walking along the waterfront soon, but not until after her other cousin—Blythe—got there from D.C. So, since her hand didn't really hurt all that much, Quinn—who'd been up since the butt-crack of dawn, as Mom would say—dragged out some of her homeschooling textbooks and did a couple of assignments, which made Mom happy, she could tell. She'd also tried playing the old piano in the gathering room, but she gave up after a couple of minutes because it was so badly out of tune she couldn't tell if she was hitting the right notes or not. So now she was poking around in one of the upstairs bedrooms, even though she kept sneezing from all the dust. It smelled funny, too. Like Mrs. Davis's—her babysitter's—apartment upstairs when she kept her windows closed for too long.

She could hear April and Mom talking downstairs again, and even though she knew it was stupid her stomach started to hurt a little. Like it used to when she'd hear Mom and Lance whispering out in the living room, right before they broke up, the words sounding all sharp and pointy, like knives—

Quinn closed her eyes, imagining she could hear her grandmother, feel her heartbeat in her ear when she'd give Quinn a hug. Grams used to say thinking too much about your past, especially the parts that make you feel bad, keeps you from seeing the good things right in front of you.

Then she heard April laugh, and she smiled. April was cool. When they'd gone to the store, April had actually listened to her. Like she cared what Quinn thought about stuff. Mom told her April's husband died, a thought that tried to make Quinn sad about Grams dying. For a while she'd been bummed about Lance, too, but she got over it. Because now that she thought about it, his smile had been all fake. Like he was trying too hard. And why Mom couldn't see that Quinn did not know.

Ryder, though—now *his* smile had made her feel like everything was really going to be okay—

Holy cannoli, her great-grandmother had so much *stuff. Everywhere.* Mom had said to be careful, there might be spiders, but Quinn liked spiders. Actually she liked bugs, period, but especially spiders, although she wasn't a total dummy, and knew to stay away from black widows. Other than that, the house was way cool, especially being so close to the water. And all that sky…

She walked over to the bedroom's dirty window, thinking she felt like…like she wasn't stuck in her body when she looked at it. Not like she was in the sky, but like the sky was in her.

As she watched, she saw a boy—around her age, maybe,

it was hard to tell from way up here—walking along the edge of the water, a large black dog galloping ahead of him, barking its head off—

"That must be Blythe!" she heard her mom call out, and Quinn tiptoed to the head of the stairs—the floors creaked really badly—then crept down a couple of steps to sit where she could see the entryway through the bannister, wishing *she* had a cat or dog or something to keep her company until life got back to normal.

Whatever the heck that meant, she thought with a sigh.

"Oh, dear God—" Blythe Broussard's perfectly smudged, smoky eyes darted around the gathering room, clearly not knowing where to focus first. "I had no idea it was this bad."

"And it's all ours, aren't we lucky ducks?" Mel grumbled as her cousin's gaze lifted to the gathering room's leprous ceiling, her multi-bangled wrists crossed over the charcoal-gray, dolman-sleeved sweater gracefully draping her angular, nearly six-foot-tall frame.

"Lucky's not exactly the word that first comes to mind," Blythe said, the sunlight fighting through the room's three large, filthy windows glancing off her spiky blond hair, the pewter-colored works of art dangling from earlobe to shoulder. Damn things had nearly lacerated Mel's cheeks when they'd hugged. "Right now I can't decide whether she hated us more or less than our mothers."

"Now, now," April said as she carted in a bamboo tray laden with teacups—real ones, not mugs—and a plate of baked goodies. "Hate is such a strong word." Honestly, between Blythe's designer glam and April's Barbie-doll vibe, Mel felt downright frumpalicious in her jeans, hoodie and Crocs. Pink and sparkly though they were. Not that Ryder had seemed to mind the night before, she thought on a what-the-heck? as she recalled the confused look in his eyes, the intensity in his voice. The way his hand shook when he touched her. And how her body had *mwa-ha-ha'd* in response...

"Yes, it is," Blythe said, flopping down in one of the chairs and jerking Mel back to the subject at hand. Although she'd never been particularly close to her aunts, apparently their grandmother had cut off April's and Blythe's mothers, as well, for various and sundry reasons....

Okay, clearly the dude wasn't married. Because he... um, no. No way. But for damn sure Mel needed to find out a salient fact or six before this phantom dinner. A thought which provoked more *mwa-ha-ha*-ing—

"At least it's a beach house," April said. "So the weathering is good, right?"

For the love of Mike, girl—focus!

"Honey, this goes way beyond weathered," Mel said, slamming shut the gate on her renegade thoughts as her gaze latched on to the dry-rotted sheers shivering like ghosts in the drafty windows. Now that she'd seen the place in the harsh light of day...oh, dear.

Then she looked at April, all twin-setty and such, a velvet headband keeping her long hair from tangling with the goodies as she set the tray on a small table nestled between a group of tatty looking chairs. As sweet and put-together as always—even as a child, she wouldn't dream of her undies not coordinating with her outties, never mind how cheap any of it was—her smile now did little to mask the sadness camped out in eyes not quite as bright as Mel remembered.

Because despite hours of catch-up conversation the night before, during which April had coaxed Mel into spilling her guts about her failed relationship with Lance, April had not been nearly as forthcoming about her own marriage, other than to admit how much she missed her husband. But if April wanted to hide whatever she was hiding behind a heaping plate of baked goods, who was Mel—insert ironic eyeroll here—to say?

"Where'd you get those?"

"I popped out to that new bakery on Main Street while you were still asleep. Y'all want coffee or tea? I've got both in the kitchen. And hot chocolate for Quinn, if she wants it."

Blythe and Mel exchanged a glance before Mel said, "What's with the perfect hostess routine?"

Artfully arranging her wares on the dinged table, April shrugged. "I like taking care of people. Makes me feel useful. So what'll it be?"

"Coffee," Mel and Blythe chorused before Mel bellowed, "Quinn! Breakfast!" which naturally got a "Who's Quinn?" from Blythe.

"Mel's little girl," April said before scurrying back to the kitchen. "Sweetest child ever..."

"Don't believe a word of it," Mel said to Blythe, selecting a muffin from the pile and settling into one of the chairs to feast. "The part about her being sweet, I mean," she amended as the child herself appeared, scrubbed her dusty palm across her butt to shake hands with Blythe and mumble hello, grab a muffin—but only after first ascertaining it wasn't contaminated with raisins—and bolt back toward the stairs.

"What are you doing up there?" Mel called after her.

"Nothin'. Exploring."

"You want hot chocolate with that?"

"No, I'm good."

Mel looked back at Blythe. "As I was saying."

Blythe chuckled, then said, "And why didn't I know you even had a kid?"

Their oldest cousin, even if only by a year, had always mother-henned her and April. To death. A more than decent trade-off, they'd finally decided, for Blythe's gleeful, detailed sharing of every adolescent rite of passage she'd scored ahead of her younger cousins. "S'okay," Mel said, biting into some kind of muffin. Oooh, oatmeal chocolate chip. Score. "April didn't know, either."

"And why is that, pray?"

Mel felt her face warm. "We hadn't spoken for, what? Two years by that point. I was hardly going to suddenly surface with that piece of news...this is pretty good," she said, pointing to the muffin. "But I can do better."

Which would have been Blythe's cue to follow Mel down a different conversational path. Had Blythe been anyone other than Blythe.

"Was there a husband?" she asked, buttering a corner of her scone, and Mel stuffed more muffin in her mouth.

"No," Mel said as April returned, bearing coffee. "What about you?"

"Do I have any kids?" Blythe shook her head. "Just as well, since the marriage experiment failed. Miserably."

"Oh, honey," April said with a touch to Blythe's shoulder before she sat, "That's too bad."

"Not really," Blythe said with a short laugh. "So," she said, clearly as eager to steer the conversation away from those pesky personal issues as Mel had been, "what are we doing about the house?"

"Since April's not on board with my initial plan," Mel said, "which involved a match and several gallons of strategically dribbled gasoline, I vote for selling. As quickly as possible. Although I suppose we have to..." She glanced around, then back at Blythe. "Do a little cleaning first."

"Can we even fit a bulldozer in here?"

"Maybe if we brought it through the French doors...?"

"Girls!" April barked. Well, yipped. "We are not going to toss this stuff without goin' through it! What if we throw out something important? Or valuable?"

"Then we'd never know, would we?" Blythe said. Then sighed at April's hurt expression. "Fine, fine. We'll..." She shuddered, setting her earring-sculptures to mad jiggling. "Sort. But I can't be here full-time, I've got clients lined up far as my iPad can see. I can maybe do some late afternoons and evenings, how's that?"

"Works for me," April said, even as Mel saw any possibility of her escaping this hell-hole in a timely manner disintegrate before her eyes. "But—"

"And I know we won't get top dollar for the place in the condition it's in," Blythe continued, "but some fresh paint might mitigate the ick factor enough to get *something* for it. I know a Realtor not too far away, I'll have her come do a market analysis early next week—"

"I don't suppose you could stage this for, like, cheap?" Mel asked.

Blythe laughed. An oh-you-poor-deluded-soul kind of titter. "Sweetie, I'm a decorator. Not God. Although some of my clients seem to think I am," she said with a grin, sipping her coffee.

"Actually..." April's baby blues bounced from one to the other. Like an adorable, fluffy kitten with serious mischief on its mind. "I thought maybe we could discuss, um, alternatives. To selling, I mean."

Another exchanged glance preceded Blythe's careful, "Such as?"

"Well...how about turning it back into an inn? Or at least a bed-and-breakfast?"

While Mel nearly choked on her bite of muffin, Blythe hooted. "Sorry, count me out. Not about to give up my life—let alone a career I busted my posterior to achieve—

to run a B&B. Anywhere. With anyone. Even you. An inn-keeper I am not. End of discussion."

Then April turned her undeterred gaze on Mel, who shook her head as vehemently as she dared while her eyes were still watering. She lifted one finger before taking a swallow of coffee, then cleared her throat. "Don't look at me, I'd rather shove sharp sticks under my fingernails than move back here."

"Why, for heaven's sake?" April said, her voice all kitteny-soft but her eyes...not. "Okay, so I get that Blythe might not be able to change *her* life, but you already said you lost your job—"

"You lost your job? Oh, sweetie..."

See, this is why she never told people stuff. Because they used it against you.

"—and an inn has to have somebody to cook. And that can't be me, because I can't even make toast. And ohmigod," April said to Blythe, "you should have tasted this stir-fry she made last night, swear to God angels sang in my mouth—"

"Stop!" Throat cleared, hands lifted, Mel leveled her gaze on her cousin. "First off, it was a simple stir-fry, for heaven's sake, I didn't even make the sauce from scratch. And second...I'm sorry, hon. I really am—" Okay, she wasn't, but she didn't have to be mean about it "—but me staying here? Not gonna happen. There are too many..." She pressed her lips together before she tripped over her big mouth right into dangerous territory. Then—hallelujah!—she realized she had the perfect out. "Besides, if Blythe isn't interested—"

"Sharp sticks? Right there with ya, babycakes."

"—then we'd have to buy out her share of the property. And I don't have a cent to spare right now." Or ever—

"Um, not a problem," April said quietly. "Because if

you're absolutely sure you don't want to go into this with me—" she looked from one to the other, getting two vigorous head shakes in response "—I could buy both of you out. And have more than enough left over for renovations." At their gape-mouthed expressions, she blushed almost as pink as Mel's Crocs. "Since my attorney tells me I'm apparently stinking rich."

It was all still a bit much to take in, Mel thought as she tossed together this and that into her version of a salade Nicoise, that the cousin who'd barely had a pot to pee in, as Nana would say, had been able to assure Blythe that, yes, a six-figure budget to renovate the old house would not be a problem.

She'd known her husband Clayton was wealthy, of course—something about a family business which he and his mother had sold some years before—but she'd had no idea how wealthy until after his death.

And she still seemed a little gobsmacked about it all, unable—or unwilling—to say much more. Probably because the poor thing was still grieving too hard, Mel mused as she sliced boiled potatoes and dumped them into the wooden salad bowl. Although April did confess that as a child, her biggest wish had been to live in the house forever. Now, to get a shot at *owning* it, to have something that was completely hers, was a dream come true—

"Whatcha making?" Quinn said as she sashayed into the kitchen and plopped into one of the chairs, all big, blue trusting eyes and ingenuous grin, and Mel's heart fisted inside her chest, the truth relentlessly lapping at her consciousness like the waves against the beach. Being around her cousins again, slipping back into the easy, open relationship that had made those childhood summers so special, so free, only made her realize how much that damn secret was holding both of them prisoner.

"Salade Nicoise," Mel said over a spurt of anger. "You hungry?"

"Starving." Puckering her forehead, Quinn snitched a piece of cold asparagus from the cutting board and popped it into her mouth. Kid always had preferred "good" food, in fact, for which Mel had always been grateful. Sweet, no. Omnivorous, yes, the raisin phobia notwithstanding. "Mom…you okay?"

"What? Oh, fine. Just tired." *Smile,* she commanded her mouth. Grudgingly, it complied. "Didn't sleep particularly well last night." As in, not at all. *Thank you, Ryder…*

"Me, neither," Quinn said. "It was so quiet I could hear my heart beating." She shuddered, then filched another piece of asparagus. "So…what's going on? Like, is Blythe gonna decorate the house or something?"

Although both Blythe and Mel remained adamant that they still wanted no part of their cousin's scheme-slash-dream, it was obvious Blythe could not wait to get her mitts on the place, even as she insisted on waiving her fee. Said having it in her portfolio was more than worth the hassle of shifting around appointments to oversee the project—which they hoped to have done before Christmas, when the annual St. Mary's Cove Festival brought in tourists by the boatload. Literally.

"April's going to keep the house and pay Blythe and me for our part of it. So, yeah, Blythe's going to make it all pretty."

Quinn's brows flew up. "Does that mean we can come visit?"

More anger spurted. Accompanied by a healthy side order of fear. "I don't know, baby."

Brows dropped. "Why? Won't April let us?"

"Of course April would let us. That's not the issue—"

"It's Ryder, isn't it?"

And didn't that testify to the sorriness of the whole situation that Quinn's assumption that *Ryder* was the issue was actually a relief? Which didn't keep Mel's eyes from snapping to her daughter's. "What?"

"You already said you two were friends. When you were kids. So how come you act so strange around him?"

"I do not—"

"Mom." Huffed sigh. "Not blind, okay? Even if I don't exactly know what I'm seeing."

"Remind me to trade you in for a dumb model, 'kay?"

"So...does that mean I'm right? It's not that we couldn't come back, it's that you don't want to. Because of Ryder."

Sighing, Mel resumed her chopping. "It's complicated."

"He's not...ohmigod—is he my *father?*"

Mel laughed. Sort of. Then turned to get something, anything, out of the fridge. "No, baby. He's not your father."

"Swear?"

"On my life."

"Was he at least your boyfriend?"

Annoyance trumping embarrassment, Mel sucked it up and carted a couple of tomatoes to the table, along with a clean cutting board. "Not my boyfriend, either. Hon, Ryder's five years older than I am. I mean, when he was sixteen I was eleven."

"Oh. Ew."

"Exactly." *And can we please move on—?*

"So how'd you two know each other?"

Apparently not. The hacked, er, wedged tomatoes dumped on top of the salad, Mel inwardly sighed. And, okay, asked a God she wasn't exactly on speed dial status with for the right words. Not for her sake, for her kid's.

And you know what? Those truth-waves lapped a little harder, eroding her resolve a little more and making her curse her grandmother for leaving her the house—or a third of it, anyway—followed by another surge of annoyance, that they hadn't simply decided to dump the place. So future visits wouldn't be even be an issue. Then there was Ryder, showing up on her doorstep…and Quinn's timing for impaling herself on that nail…and her grandmother's lawyer spilling the beans…

Yep, this here was what you might call a perfect cluster…fluff.

The salad assembled, Mel set it aside—she'd do the dressing after the others showed their faces—and sat across from the little girl she'd sworn to protect with her last dying breath.

"Grams and your grandfather worked for Ryder's parents. Grams was the housekeeper and cook, my father was the groundskeeper."

Quinn's jaw dropped. "Really?"

"Really. We lived in a cute little cottage—" after a fashion "—on their property. After I was born, Ryder sort of appointed himself my honorary big brother."

"Why?"

Because that's Ryder. "You'd have to ask him that." Oh, hell. "I don't mean literally ask him, I just mean…"

"I know what you mean. Geez." Quinn stood to reach across the table and grab a tomato, cramming it into her mouth before she said around it, "So why'd you stop being friends?"

"Our lives changed," Mel said over her thumping heart. "We got older, he went on to college and—after my dad died—Grams and I moved to Baltimore."

"When was this?"

"Before you were born."

"And that's it?"

"Pretty much."

Quinn gave her a funny look, then shrugged. "For what it's worth? He seems really nice."

There was no mistaking the wistfulness in her voice. That cross between don't-want-to-be-hurt-again caution and sweet, sanguine hope…

Mel plucked out the unfinished thought before it could take root. "He's a doctor, he's supposed to be nice."

"Yeah, right. You remember the doc in the E.R. when I broke my wrist? Worst. Attitude. Ever—"

Her cousins' arrival at that moment blessedly ejected Dr. Ryder Caldwell from the conversation, if not the look in her daughter's eyes that said this discussion wasn't over yet. Not by a long shot.

Oh, yeah. She was fluffed, all right.

Chapter Five

Ryder rang Amelia's doorbell, telling himself it was only professional courtesy motivating him to stop by to make sure Quinn's stitches were healing up okay. But he knew that was a lie. As would Mel. Smart cookie, that Mel. Not to mention enough of a worrywart about her daughter that she would have called him if there was a problem.

This was dumb, he should just leave now—

"Oh!" said the tall, graceful blonde who answered the door, flashing him a full body scan before planting one long-fingered hand on a hip that was nothing but bone and dusty denim. A grin sliced her angular face as Betty Crocker aromas slithered from behind her. "Ryder?"

"Holy cow...Blythe?"

She laughed, then waved him in, her voluminous, blue-gray sweater sliding off one shoulder. After calling for Mel, she turned eyes nearly the same color on him, swiping at a smudge of dirt on her cheek. "My, my, my," she said on a low chuckle as she tucked a pointy wisp of nearly white hair behind one multi-studded ear. "After spending all day surrounded by rampant decay—" she swept one arm to indicate, he assumed, the decrepit state of the house "—you are a sight for sore eyes. Nice to see that at least *something* in this two-bit town actually improved over the last decade!"

Ryder smiled, even as he bristled at the dig. Of all the places he'd lived or visited, St. Mary's was still home, the place he'd deliberately chosen to establish his career. A point he might've been tempted to make had Mel not appeared, about a hundred expressions zipping across her face and pinking her cheeks. Which in turn made her eyes look brighter and Ryder realize that the big brother thing was definitely not working for him anymore.

She'd pulled her hair back into a ponytail—blast from the past—so she was all dark, messy, sexy bangs and big, pale, wary eyes. And those pink cheeks. But mostly the wary eyes.

"Hey," he said, "Thought I'd check on Quinn." From underneath a deep pink cardigan a lowish-cut white top hinted at cleavage, clung to what caused the cleavage. He looked up. Just in time to catch the arched eyebrow. "See how she's doing."

Aaaand time went into stop-action mode.

Blythe cleared her throat, backing away while jabbing a thumb over her shoulder. "And if you'll excuse me, I've got a hot date with an upstairs closet...."

They both watched Blythe's retreat, dust motes boogying around them for several seconds until Mel raked a hand through her bangs, provoking memories. "Quinn's fine."

"And that would be your professional medical opinion."

"After ten years of on-the-job training? As good as." Ryder lowered his chin; Mel sighed, said, "Fine, see for yourself." Then, with a nod toward the kitchen, she turned. "We've been making cookies."

Speaking of clinging…no mom jeans for this gal. And could we hear a hallelujah for that?

No, what he needed was someone or something to clobber some sense into him, stat. So Mel was back and they were all grown up now and he no longer had to feel like scum because he was physically attracted to her. Except he still did because this was *Mel* and the timing was no better now than it had been then, legal issues aside, and because, hello? Not…ready? Willing? Able?

Okay, *able,* maybe. Probably. But he still wouldn't feel right about it. Hell, even without the clobbering he knew this whole thing had *disaster in the making* written all over it.

And yet.

In the eclectically furnished dining room they passed a dusty-glassed, dark wood breakfront crammed with crystal and china, the matching buffet laden with tarnished silver. Good, if neglected, pieces at odds with the general tattiness of the rest of the furnishings.

"What happened to the other stuff? On the buffet?"

"Boxed. Pitched. Whatever."

"So…you guys going to hold an estate sale?"

"Haven't decided yet. Right now we're just trying to figure out what stays and what goes."

"Stays?"

Mel slowed enough for Ryder to see her mouth pull flat. "We're not selling. Or I should say, April's not selling. She wants to keep the place, turn it into a B&B. So she's buying Blythe and me out and turning it into something people might actually want to spend the night in."

"Oh. And how do you feel about that?"

"Resigned," she said after a moment. "And relieved, I

suppose. That I can walk away and never think about this place again—"

"Ryder!" From the kitchen table where she'd apparently been decorating cookies, Quinn grinned up at him, and from out of nowhere Ryder felt knifed, that she didn't know who he really was. Who *she* really was, for that matter. "Did you come to make sure my hand's okay?"

"I did." Shaking off the unsettled feeling—for the moment—he glanced around, taking in the supplement-divested counters, now smothered with plates of cookies in all shapes and varieties. "Although something tells me I needn't have bothered. That thing still works?" he asked, frowning at the stove.

"After a fashion," Mel said, then sighed, taking in the cookie explosion. "We might've gone a little overboard."

"You think?"

"That's because we couldn't decide what kind to make," Quinn said, then wagged her bandaged hand. "It doesn't even hurt, I swear."

"Glad to hear it," Ryder said, sitting at right angles to her. "But why don't you let me take a peek, anyway?"

"Knock yourself out," she said, extending her hand in a very royal gesture, and Ryder smiled, even as the knife twisted again, although for another reason.

He glanced up at Mel, who was concentrating on her daughter's hand, and way too many emotions collided in his brain to suss out. But one thing was absolutely clear—for both Mel's and her daughter's sake, this subterfuge needed to end, now. Or at least very soon. Because not only could he tell the whole situation was eating Mel alive, but the longer Quinn was kept in the dark, the worse it would be when she found out the truth.

And she would find out. Because these things always worked their way to the surface. Always.

A minute later, satisfied, he replaced the gauze with an antiseptic plastic bandage and gave Quinn a thumb's up, then Mel a grin which he didn't feel nearly as much as he would have liked.

"I do good work, if I say so myself," he said, and she sputtered a short laugh.

"Me, too," Quinn said, planting her hands on the edge of the table and pushing herself to her feet, giving Mel what sure as heck to Ryder looked like a pointed look. "C'n I take some cookies up to my room?"

Mel handed her an enormous plastic mixing bowl. "Go for it."

With a squeal, the child gathered enough cookies to feed Delaware and flounced out of the room, munching as she marched. Figuring whatever was left was fair game, Ryder plucked a still-warm oatmeal cookie from a plate in the center of the table. "Now you've gone and done it," he said to Mel's back as, with much clattering and banging, she washed several discolored, misshapen cookie trays at the chipped sink. "I may never leave. At least not until the cookies are gone."

The cookie sheets haphazardly stacked in a dingy plastic drying rack on the counter, Mel turned, drying her hands on an equally dingy towel, and Ryder suddenly flashed back to another kitchen, another woman drying her hands on a towel, smiling at the two kids sitting at the kitchen table, stuffing their faces with her oatmeal cookies. Odd, how easy things seemed back then.

At least, for him.

Ryder held up another cookie. "Your mom's recipe?"

He saw the flash of pain in her eyes before she nodded. "Although she didn't bake much after, um, we left. Or cook, either. Said she just didn't feel like it, with Dad not there. So I learned in self-defense." Her mouth pulled into a sly grin. "As you may have noticed, I'm not exactly a three-carrot-slices-on-a-lettuce-leaf kind of girl."

"I noticed." She rolled her eyes, provoking another memory flash, even though now, with a pang, Ryder saw it for the illusion it was. Chewing, he regarded the cookie with a gaze that probably bordered on worshipful. "I'm guessing you use real butter?"

Her eyes actually dilated. "Every chance I get. Well, um…" The towel slung over a door knob, she crossed her arms. "I've already played hooky with the cookie baking, I really need to get back to sorting and cataloguing. We only have Blythe through tomorrow, she has to get back to D.C.—"

"Need help?"

"Don't be—"

"Unless you *want* to spend the rest of your life going through your grandmother's things? Come on," he said, getting to his feet and yanking open the nearest cupboard door. "It'll be fun."

"In what universe?"

"Mine."

"You honestly have nothing better to do?"

He hefted a stack of chipped stoneware onto the counter, his heart pounding at the prospect of bringing up a subject he'd lay odds she was not even remotely ready to discuss. "It's Saturday. So not really, no."

"You do realize how lame that sounds?"

"And *you* realize," he said, clunking a second stack onto the counter, "the longer you stand here arguing with me the longer it'll take to get away again?"

He felt her eyes on the side of his face for a long moment before, huffing a sigh, she opened the cupboard door on the other side of the sink and started pulling out glasses, no two of which appeared to match. At her extended silence, he said, "You going to tell me what's bugging you or let me guess?"

"For God's sake, Ry…" She faced him again, a deep furrow between her brows. "What do you want?"

"From you?"

"Sure. Let's start there."

He grinned. "Dinner?"

She rolled her eyes. "Still thinking."

The smile dimmed. "Then…to regain your trust?"

The question mark at the end of his answer startled him more than it apparently did Mel, even though another flush washed over her cheeks as she turned back to pull out more glasses. "That might be tricky since I'm not really sure I completely trust anyone anymore," she said, and he felt like he'd been sucker-punched.

"Don't you sometimes wish," he said carefully, "that you could get a do-over?"

"No. Never. Especially if it meant I'd have to live through the same crap."

"But if it didn't?"

"Then there'd undoubtedly be different crap to live through. Right?" With a grimace, she tossed several of the glasses into a plastic-lined bin where they sadly shattered, their lives finally over. "Life is just…crappy."

"You didn't used to be so bitter."

"People change." Another glass met its demise.

"You're just in a bad place right now—"

"Now?" Her gaze lanced his. "You can't even begin to imagine what the last ten years has been like for me, Ryder. What my life has been like. Okay, I'm not saying it's all been horrible, that would be a gross exaggeration and totally unfair to people who've faced far worse challenges. Not to mention…I can't imagine not having Quinn. How could I possibly regret *her?* But still. Most days I feel

like I'm shoveling sand—I no sooner plug up one problem than another one appears, and the thing of it is, it's my own damn fault—" She abruptly turned away. "None of which is any of your concern. Sorry."

"For dumping on me?"

She shrugged, then dragged over a chair, climbing up on it to reach the upper shelves.

"Hey. If you can't dump on me, then who?"

"And you do not want to get me started on the folly that is letting myself lean on other people."

"Especially people who let you down when you needed them most, you mean."

"Or who might have hidden agendas. Good God, there's a dead bug the size of my head in here."

Ryder frowned. "Where on earth did that come from?"

"I'm thinking Jersey. Oh. You mean the agenda comment?" With a shudder, she swept the carcass off the shelf onto the counter. She hadn't been kidding—*biiiig* sucker. "The deep, dark recesses of my embittered brain." Her gaze met his. "Forgive me for being skeptical, but…" She lowered her voice. "Is your wanting to reconnect really about me, or about my daughter?"

"Are you deliberately trying to piss me off?"

"Is it working?"

"Heck, yeah, it's working. Wanting to patch things up with you and wanting to get to know Quinn are two separate issues, even if they're intertwined—"

"And what if I don't *want* to 'patch things up'? Because that's all it would be, some…some jury-rigged approximation of something that died a natural death more than ten years ago. And would have in any case," she said before he could protest.

"You don't know that," he said, and her brows flew up.

"Oh, really? What? You would have waited for me to

grow up? I mean, come on, Ryder—do you honestly expect me to believe you were saving yourself for me after you went off to school?" When he flushed, she let out a harsh laugh. "No, I didn't think so. And even after that night, even considering you *didn't* know what happened…you could have found me if you'd wanted to, it wouldn't have been that hard. But you didn't because, hello? That chapter in our lives…it was over. You'd moved on. And don't even think about apologizing for doing what you were supposed to do. Or for simply being a guy. Although that does beg the question—so why *are* you still single?"

"What?"

"You heard me. You're over thirty and straight and a *doctor,* for the love of Pete. No way have you made it this far unscathed. So, c'mon. Spill."

No, he sure hadn't. And everything she'd said…she was right, of course. As much as he'd valued their friendship, they had been kids, Ryder hadn't planned at the time on returning to St. Mary's and Mel sure as hell hadn't planned on sticking around. Part of the reason, he supposed, he'd let go—because, as she'd said, there would have been no point.

And there were no words for how little he wanted to talk about this. Because, God, it hurt. Like a sonuvabitch.

But without being totally open, what hope did he have of regaining her trust?

The dishes temporarily forgotten, he clamped his hands on the counter edge and blew out a long breath. "You're absolutely right, there were…others."

"Thank God, you had me worried there for a minute—"

"In fact, I was engaged," he said, taking an almost perverse pleasure in her flinch of surprise, even as the admission ripped open the barely healed wound all over again.

* * *

Well, you asked, dumbbutt, Mel thought, only to swallow hard when she saw the pain briefly flash across his face. A pain she suspected he didn't let a lot of people see.

"Was?"

"She died," he said softly, not looking at her, and Mel lost her breath.

"Holy hell, Ry—when?"

"Last year. A month before our wedding. Car accident," he said with a slight roll of his shoulders, a guy-trying-to-be-brave shrug she'd witnessed before, when some chickie or other in high school had done him wrong and he'd tried so hard to pretend it didn't matter.

This, though…crap. Because for all she'd meant every word about how tough things had been, that she was bitter and cynical and knew that rainbows were an illusion, that didn't mean she didn't care. Or couldn't feel anybody else's misery.

Especially Ryder's.

As a kid she'd watched him limp in from a soccer game, filthy and bleeding and grinning, heard him stand up to his mother without so much as a quaver in his voice, but when it came to romance damned if he didn't have the most tender, vulnerable heart of any male she'd ever known. That he'd suffered deeply—was still suffering—was more than evident in his wracked expression, and it made her feel like she'd swallowed lye.

Except then he gave her one of those pierce-her-soul looks and said, "No pity. Got it?"

Never mind that all she wanted was to take him in her arms and hug him for, oh, the next ten years. Instead she climbed off the chair, dragging over a box to pack the "better" stuff in until they decided what to do with it. "So riddle me this, Batman," she said, her gaze carefully averted, "since it's obvious you're still hurting, why are you looking at me like I'm, um, a girl?"

Loooong pause. Then, behind her: "Not a girl, honey. Not by a long shot. A woman."

Her eyes cut to his, saw something she couldn't/ wouldn't/so did not want to handle and skittered away again. "Not answering the quest—"

"Because you're gorgeous and I'm *not* dead. Although I sure as hell felt like it until I saw you again."

Mel dumped two glasses into the box a little hard, breaking one of them. Not that this was a loss. "I see."

"I doubt it—"

"I know how hurting men act," she said, wheeling on him. "How they seek...solace—"

"And not to be crude, but if that's what I was looking for I certainly wouldn't seek it from you." When she barked out a laugh, he let his head drop back, then sighed. "That didn't come out right. I meant, if that's *all* I was looking for, I could find it easily enough from other sources. As it is I've had absolutely no interest in even casual dating since...then."

Mel raised her brows, waiting. Ryder sighed.

"Do I find you appealing?" His eyes darkened. "Oh, yeah. Am I going to act on that?" He shook his head. "Because it would be—"

"Wrong," Mel finished, then marched the broken glass pieces across the kitchen to dump them in the garbage.

"I'm not making any sense, am I?"

"Not a whole lot, no."

He picked up the top to a cow-shaped butter dish and skimmed his fingers along its back. "When I heard you were back, I didn't know what to expect. How I'd react, seeing you again. And to be honest I still haven't sorted it all out. But when I talk about wanting a do-over..."

He set down the top, his forehead crunched. "I don't mean literally. Obviously. God, I wouldn't want to be that kid again for anything. Let alone that frustrated, horny kid who didn't dare follow through on what he was thinking. But being around you again…it makes me remember a time when things were good. For me, anyway. I know— now—they probably weren't so good for you."

She could lie. Heaven knew she'd had enough practice at it. Except she was tired of lying. Damned tired. "When we hung out together, things were good for me, too. Good enough, anyway."

His smile was sad. "I thought I'd stopped missing you. Apparently I was wrong."

Oh, hell. She was going to cry. And that would never do. "Well," she said, after way too long a pause and in a voice she knew wasn't kidding anybody, "isn't that corny as hell?" and Ryder held out his arm and whispered, "C'mere, you."

And instead of running shrieking from the room like, you know, a sane person, she went, and he slung an arm around her shoulders and pulled her close, and it didn't feel nearly as bizarre as she might have assumed it would. In fact, it felt *pret*-ty good. Which of course wasn't good at all.

Especially when Ryder said, "Still friends?" and Mel sighed, knowing that despite all her protests, all her determination to pretend what they'd had as kids was dead and buried…it wasn't. Worse, though—much, much worse— was the what-could-be threatening to eclipse the what-had-been.

Because nothing ranked higher on the old follymeter than *two* people with broken hearts.

So she pulled away, or would have if Ryder hadn't caught her hand, forcing her gaze to his, and oh, dear merciful heavens, was the dude conflicted, or what? Maybe even more than she was, and that was going some.

"Ryder—"

"Because I've got a lot of making up to do."

Her brows slammed together. "I didn't ask—"

"You didn't have to."

She removed her hand and crossed her arms, his touch still making her palm tingle. Among other things. Because, fine, she'd missed him, too, whether she'd let herself think about that or not, and now that she was a grownup and knew how everything worked—and how much fun it was when they did—simply looking at the man made her entire body hum quite the merry little tune.

"I already told you," she said over the humming, "I'm totally over what happened between us. So no making up to do—"

"But you're definitely not over what my family did to you."

She almost laughed. "*You* can't make up for that."

"I sure as hell can try," he said, then stooped to snag her gaze in his. "You need a friend, Mel," he said, adding, when her mouth opened, "for Quinn's sake, if nothing else. Because it's not good, keeping all of this jammed up inside you. And I know the last thing you'd want to do is take out your frustration on your child."

"I would never do that!"

"You really want to take that chance?"

No, she didn't. Because—damn his hide—he was right. Already there'd been times when she'd been short with Quinn for no reason other than not having an outlet for all the junk bubbling inside her head. Even before her mother's death, she'd been loath to vent to the woman whose life had been turned upside down because of Mel's sketchy judgment. And if nothing else, Ryder had always understood her. Or at least, did a good job of pretending he did.

Which, perhaps, was what she'd missed most.

What scared her the most, too.

"And you know what?" Ryder said. "I could use a friend, too."

She hazarded a glance in his direction. "Even a temporary one?"

His grin shattered her heart. "I'm very good at working with what I'm given. Now. You got a box for these plates, or should we toss them?"

Quinn had just come down the back staircase and into the pantry when she saw Ryder take Mom's hand. She'd been so startled she'd frozen, not sure what to do. Although tiptoeing away had been pretty high on the list.

But then she'd caught bits and pieces of their conversation and she *couldn't* leave. Because nobody ever told kids anything. Or at least, not as much as there was to tell. Especially Mom, who considering the eleventy billion times she'd told Quinn she could tell *her* anything, sure as heck didn't seem interested in returning the favor.

So she'd ducked behind the wall outside the doorway, straining to hear what they were saying, her heart thumping like crazy that she'd get caught. Only the longer she listened, the more confused she got. What did Ryder mean, what his family had done to Mom? Keeping all of *what* jammed up inside her? And what did any of it have to do with Quinn?

Unfortunately, one problem with hearing a conversation you weren't supposed to was that you couldn't exactly ask for an explanation afterwards. Poop. But eventually Ryder and Mom went back to talking about dumb stuff, so Quinn scooted back upstairs, where she ran into April at the end of the hallway, her arms full of sheets.

"Hey there, baby girl." April dumped the sheets into a big box by the linen closet, waving her hand at the cloud of dust before giving Quinn a big smile. "Whatcha doing?"

"Nothing, I…" She glanced back toward the stairs, her face getting all hot.

"Hey…everything okay?"

No, it sure as heck wasn't, and that was a fact. Quinn frowned at her cousin. "If I ask you something, you promise not to say anything to my mom?"

After like half a second, April took Quinn by the elbow and marched her into the nearest bedroom, nodding toward a stuffed chair in the corner with ugly blue flowers all over it. She partially shut the door with her hip, then sat on the edge of the bed, although you couldn't pay Quinn to get anywhere near that yucky old bedspread. "I can't promise that whatever you tell me I won't discuss with your mama, that would depend on what it is. So you might want to think about that before we go any further. But if you need to run whatever it is by me first—like a rehearsal—I'm here for you. Okay?"

Quinn nodded, then decided if she didn't let it all out she'd pop. Looping a curl around her index finger, she shrank into the chair, not sure if she felt worse for what she'd done, what she'd heard, or that she was dragging April—whom she hardly knew—into it. But finally she whispered, "I kinda overhead my mom and Ryder in the kitchen, talking. I didn't mean to, I swear, I just went to get a glass of milk and…"

Shaking her head, she let go of the curl to fold her hands in her lap and look down at them. "Ryder's family…I know my grandparents worked for them and stuff, but Ryder said something about…wanting to make up for what they did to Mom. Do you know what he's talking about?"

April's eyebrows about lifted right off her head. "No, baby, I sure don't. I swear. He say anything else?"

"Not really, no. Not about that, anyway. But…I also saw them holding hands."

"Who? Your mama and Ryder?"

"Yeah."

"Oh." April touched the little gold necklace she always wore. "Um…you know they were real good friends when they were kids, right?"

"Yeah. Mama told me. But if you ask me he was not looking at her like a friend. I mean, they were *talking* about being friends, but…" Quinn pushed out a breath. "Something's going on, April, I know it. Something nobody wants me to know. Things just don't feel right." She smushed her lips together. "And they haven't for a long time."

"Don't feel right, how?"

"I don't know. But ever since I was little it's been like…" She let her eyes fall to her lap again, almost ashamed to say what she was thinking. "Like Mom's not telling me the truth."

After a couple of seconds, April said, real quietly, "Honey, look at me." When Quinn finally did, a tear dribbling down her cheek, April leaned over to take Quinn's hand. "Your mama and I haven't been close in a long time, so I'm as clueless as you are, what any of that meant. I'll tell you one thing, though—she loves you with all her heart, and she would die before hurting you. Or letting you get hurt. So my advice to you, sweet thing, is to come right out and tell her what you told me. You don't have to mention what you heard, or how you heard it, only that things are feeling a little strange and you'd like to know what's going on."

"So you think something *is* going on?"

"I didn't say that. But I do know…" She paused. "People—and everybody does this at some time or another, so don't feel bad—we hear part of a conversation and get to wondering about it, and before you know it we're making ourselves nuts, filling in the blanks with all sorts of things that only exist in our heads. And I know your mama would feel awful if she knew how confused you were right now. I bet she has no idea."

"So you think I should be honest with her?"

"Don't see any other way of getting answers, do you?"

Quinn nodded, feeling both better and more jumbled up at the same time. *Figure that one out,* she thought with a sigh.

By Sunday evening Mel had to admit that although they weren't done yet—not by a long shot, they'd barely sorted out the dining and gathering rooms—they'd made a lot more progress than she would've thought possible in only two days with three women whose takes varied greatly on what was worth keeping and what wasn't.

However, they not only muddled through without bloodshed, but there was a big old Dumpster in the driveway chock-full of crap not even worth donating. So go, them. Whatever April wanted to keep—the good china and crystal, a few pieces of furniture Blythe said would look terrific once reupholstered or refinished—would eventually get shoved into one of the downstairs bedrooms, the rest carted off to various charity thrift stores.

Which meant April would be more or less starting from scratch, a prospect that clearly excited her no end. In fact, after Blythe declared herself too exhausted to haul her butt back to D.C. that night, and that she'd get an early start in the morning, April had spent the better part of the evening blissfully poring over—and over—their cousin's first sketchy draft of the proposed kitchen remodel, currently laid out on the to-be-refinished dining table. Which is where Mel found her after tucking in Quinn for the night.

"She go down okay?" April asked, taking a sip of her tea from the mug hugged close to her chest and looking about ten years old with her hair pulled into twin pony-tails, her size 5 Mary Janes peeking out from her flared leg jeans. She, too, was headed back to Richmond in the morning, but only long enough to pack up her clothes and put Clayton's house on the market. While Mel didn't rel-ish the idea of it just being her and Quinn in the great big house, she'd promised to stay and continue chipping away at the upstairs bedrooms. And then there was the attic, which they'd glanced at, groaned, and quietly closed the door to again. Mel wouldn't be surprised to find the re-mains of Union soldiers up there.

Now she released a tired laugh. Every muscle in her body ached, although she was grateful she'd been too busy to mull over that "let's be friends" convo with Ryder, too tired at night to do anything but zonk out within seconds of hitting her bed. "She's ten. Not ten months. She likes to read herself to sleep."

"Not that this will come as a shock, I'm sure," her cousin said with a grin, "but I'm crazy about that kid."

"Yeah. Me, too."

Smiling, Mel dragged herself into the kitchen for a cookie—or three—to find Blythe standing at the counter, slumming it in a ratty T-shirt and ripped jeans as she pol-ished off the leftover casserole, warmed up to go with the slow-cooker pork roast Mel decided to make after Blythe unearthed a still-in-its-box Crock-Pot at the bottom of the hall closet, of all places. Blythe's gaze swung from Mel to April, who'd trailed in behind Mel, shutting the swinging door behind her. When she crossed the room to push closed the door to the back stairs as well, Mel felt the back of her neck prickle.

"What's going on?"

With a sigh, April sat at the table, focused on her tea. Mel offered her a plate of cookies, but she shook her head. "I'm still stuffed from dinner. And I'll have you know I've never eaten three servings of cauliflower in my life."

"There's cauliflower in here?" Blythe said. "My brain shorted out at the bacon."

"And cheese," April said on another sigh. "You *sure* I can't talk you into—?"

"Positive," Mel said. "Not that I don't think if anybody can make this work, it'd be you. But count me out." Although she had to admit she wasn't relishing the idea of job-hunting when she got back to Baltimore. And/or making five gazillion bacon-wrapped shrimp appetizers for weddings every weekend. Not to mention Blythe's plans for the kitchen were...intriguing. But enough of that. "And I'm guessing you didn't close the doors so nobody would hear you extolling the virtues of my cauliflower casserole."

The cousins exchanged another glance before April took a cookie, anyway, nibbling at the edge for a moment before asking, "Has Quinn...talked to you?"

"Talked to me? Are you kidding, the kid never shuts up." Again with the glances. And the prickles. "Okay, guys—what's this about?"

Blythe burped the circa 1972 Tupperware container and turned, her hands braced on the edge of the counter behind her. "She came to April yesterday. While Ryder was here."

"And I thought I'd convinced her that she needed to bring up the subject herself," April said. "With you, I mean. But..."

She looked to Blythe, who pushed herself away from

the counter and pulled out a kitchen chair. "But since she hasn't...well. You should probably sit."

Mel looked from one to the other, trying to make sense of what they were saying. "For God's sake, you're scaring me—what the *hell* is going on?"

"That's what your daughter wants to know," April said, and Mel's gaze zinged to hers. "Believe me, I didn't ask to get in the middle of this, but she seems to think there's something you're not telling her?"

Ouch.

For all the catching-up chitchat they'd shared over the past forty-eight hours, Mel had handily diverted the conversation away from the subject of her daughter's paternity, partly because what her cousins didn't know they couldn't inadvertently let slip to certain small parties, and partly because Mel simply hadn't wanted to get into it with them.

Just like when she'd been a kid, she realized, when self-protection had made her keep things to herself—a knee-jerk reaction, she supposed, to always feeling relegated to the sidelines—even though neither of her cousins had ever given her cause to not trust them. Or think they'd judge her.

Any more than there was reason to believe they'd judge her now.

Finally she lowered herself into the chair, her fingers closing around April's when her cousin reached for her hand.

Then she pushed the plate of cookies toward her cousins. "It's a long story. You might need fortification."

An obscene amount of consumed cookies later, Blythe was all for an impromptu road trip to New York to drag Jeremy back by his 'nads to atone for his scumbaggery—a plan even sweet April appeared to consider for a moment before shaking her head. Even as she regarded Mel with genuine concern.

"My Lord, honey…what a fiasco."

"Tell me about it." Her stomach rebelling against all the sugar and butter—there was a first—Mel got up for a glass of milk. "Why on earth I even agreed to such a stupid scheme, I have no idea. And why the Caldwells thought it would work…" She shoved the milk carton back onto the shelf; the fridge wobbled when she slammed shut the door.

"You were scared, sugar," April said. "You didn't think you had any choice. And nobody's gonna fault you for doing what you did."

"Oh, yeah? What do you think my daughter's going to think when she finds out?"

Blythe stood and stretched, her hands propped on her lower back. "That you're the mom from hell, what else?" When Mel shot her a daggered look, Blythe shrugged. "She will get over it, sweetie."

"Providing I ever figure out how to give her something to get over."

"So you do want to tell her the truth?"

"What I want, is for this stupid secret to magically disappear. And, yes, I know that's not going to happen, but the *truth* is, her father's family wanted nothing to do with her. And since it's been more than ten years and they apparently still don't…" Mel forked her hands through her loose hair, then let them slap back onto the table. "At this point I honestly don't give a damn about what they'd think, or how they'd react. What are they going to do, sue me for breach of contract? And I know the longer I put this off the worse it's going to be. But…"

Blythe slipped a hand onto Mel's back to gently rub between her shoulder blades. "But you can't bear the thought of Quinn getting caught in the crossfire."

"Exactly."

"Does Ryder know?"

"He does now. But only because our grandmother died, bringing me inconveniently back to St. Mary's."

Blythe's hand stilled. "You're kidding—his parents didn't even tell him?"

"Nope. And God knows Jeremy didn't. You need somebody to ride shotgun with you on that road trip, Ry's your guy."

"Then there's your answer," April said.

"Letting Ry kill his brother?"

"Aside from that. Did he know when he came here that first night? After Quinn hurt herself?"

"Yes. Nana's lawyer had apparently told Ryder's dad we'd inherited the house. And he apparently thought it best to forewarn Ryder about Quinn."

"So the secret's beginning to unravel at the edges, anyway."

Mel's mouth pulled tight. "At one edge, anyway. But that makes things even trickier. That Quinn and Ryder have already met. She already adores him—"

"And he, her," April said. "Meaning I bet he'll do anything to help you straighten this out." Mel covered her eyes, groaning. "No, really. Let Ryder be the go-between. Especially since I assume he's not exactly pleased with his parents right now." April grinned. "And since from what little I observed I'm guessing Quinn's not the only one Ryder's keen to bond with."

At Blythe's snort, April turned on her cousin. "Don't you snort at me, Blythe Broussard. It's perfectly obvious Ryder's still got a thing for Mel."

Mel raised her hand. "Um, actually—"

"And now that you're all grown up," April said to Mel,

"he could actually do something about it. And so could you."

"No, you don't understand—"

"And we've already established how sweet you were on him that last summer we were all together. So this is a no-brainer, right?"

Momentarily giving up on wedging reality into the conversation, Mel looked at Blythe. "It was really that obvious?"

Her cousin laughed, and Mel sighed. Then Blythe said, "Although forgive me for being the voice of reason, but unlike Miss Stars-in-the-Eyes here, I'm not seeing this end well. Yeah, fine, maybe it would work to have him be the mediator between you and his parents, but anything else?" She shook her head. "Take my advice, don't even go there. Because no way this isn't all going to blow up in everybody's faces—"

"For heaven's sake," April said, soundlessly slapping her delicate little hand on the table. "Stop being so darn cynical—"

"*Guys!* Sheesh!" Mel clunked her empty glass on the counter. "April, sorry, but I'm with Blythe on this one. This really is a non-starter. About me and Ryder, I mean. Even if his fiancée hadn't died last year—"

April sucked in a little breath. "Ohmigod, you're kidding?"

"Nope. And he's still grieving. Then there's the little issue of my not being exactly gung ho about jumping into another relationship after my own disaster—"

"But maybe you're exactly what Ryder needs to heal," April said, and Blythe groaned out, "Oh, for pity's sake..."

"April! Not. Happening. Because no matter how this thing gets resolved—assuming that it does, which is not a given—do you really think I'd ever want a connection with that family again after what they did to me? To Quinn?"

"Not even with Ryder? But that's so unfair!"

"Dammit, April—nothing about *any* of this is fair! And you know something else?" she said, getting to her feet. "Nobody can figure out how to handle this but me, because I'm the one who bungled everything to begin with. So if you'll excuse me, it's late, and I'm about to fall over, so I'll see you two in the morning."

But before she got to the door, Blythe called to her. When Mel turned back, her cousins were standing side by side, both with their arms crossed, both clearly loaded for bear.

"First off," Blythe said, "so help me if I *ever* hear you take the entire blame for this on yourself, ever again, I will bitchslap you clear into next week."

"Yeah. What she said," April said, and Mel got all teary. Honestly, she was getting as bad as April.

"Thanks, guys—"

Blythe's hand flew up. "Not done yet. Quinn's your daughter, so of course it's ultimately your call. But, sweetie, this is your chance to resolve something that's obviously worrying you to death. And my guess is you're going to beat yourself up even more if you leave St. Mary's *without* resolving it. One way or the other."

Mel's mouth popped open, only to clamp shut again. Because her cousin was right. Eleven years ago she'd left because she'd felt she'd had no choice. This time the choice was hers—to continue running from the lie, or face it head on.

To—okay, might as well be honest—dodge her feelings about Ryder, or to face them head on, as well.

"Call Ryder, sweetie," Blythe said, as April bobble-headed beside her.

Agita, Mel thought on a long sigh. *I has it.*

Chapter Six

Monday decided to be one of those blue-skied, Indian-summer days that lured people outdoors. Or, in this case, prompted Ryder's father to invite Ryder to join him for lunch at a little café not far from the clinic, housed in what had originally been an eighteenth-century tavern. St. Mary's was nothing if not riddled with historic vibes. And, this time of year, sleepy to the point of comatose. Even the gulls that normally pestered the hell out of everyone during the height of the summer season couldn't be bothered to venture the few blocks inland.

But the sun was warm and the breeze balmy, so Ryder and David took advantage of the gulls' disinterest to dine al fresco in the deserted courtyard adjacent to the restaurant, even though Ryder knew not even the peaceful setting would soothe his jangled nerves.

"Beautiful day," his father said, tucking into his chicken

salad sandwich and not looking at Ryder. "Hard to believe winter's right around the corner."

"Happens every year," Ryder said, and his father smiled. Still gazing across the street at one of the many antiques shops lining Main Street, he said, "So. Have you met the child yet?"

Well, well.

Despite his father's being the one to alert him to Mel's return, since the subject had pointedly not surfaced during family dinner the day before, Ryder had assumed it would be up to him to broach it. But only with Mel's permission, which he'd yet to figure out how to get. Just like she'd yet to agree to have dinner with him.

"Yes, actually," he said, wiping his mouth with his napkin and studying his father's profile. "She hurt herself that first night, needed some stitches. I happened to be around."

His father's eyes cut to his. "So you went over there after you talked to us."

"Did you think I wouldn't?"

David looked away again. "What's she like?" he asked, and Ryder saw it, the chink in the armor. A chink he imagined had always been there, now wrenched wide open by the knowledge that his granddaughter was barely a mile away.

"She looks like Jeremy," Ryder said, and his father pressed his lips together. "But she's smart like Mel. Curious about everything. Funny. Bit of a smartass." He paused, then said, "You'd love her."

"I bet I would." He pushed his plate away. "And Mel? How is she?"

"Angry," Ryder said simply, his gut twisting that his family had done this to her, turned the always smiling girl he'd known into someone he almost didn't recognize. Except he knew—or had to believe, at least—that she was still there, underneath all that disillusionment. "She's also coming off a relationship that ended badly, which isn't exactly adding to her good mood at the moment."

"I swear to you, it wasn't my idea—"

"I know. But that doesn't change anything. The damage is done. And this isn't something that can be fixed with a dose of antibiotics or a few stitches. Good God, Dad—what were you and Mom *thinking?*"

Judging from the wounded look in his father's eyes, Ryder's blow hit its mark dead on. David ripped open two packets of sugar, dumping them in his iced tea as sparrows twittered in the Virginia-creeper-choked trellises nearby. "And I suppose you want to tell Jeremy. That you've seen her."

"Crap's gonna hit the fan eventually, Dad. And whether *I* tell him or not," he said, watching his father stir his tea, "Jeremy is an adult. Now, at least. And he will deal." Ryder paused. "And so will Mom. Man," he said with a dry laugh and a short shake of his head, "she's pulled some doozies over the years, but this one takes the cake—"

"It's not as if we completely turned our backs!" David said, clattering the teaspoon onto the edge of his plate. "We have been supporting the child all these years—"

"You bought Mel off! And making sure the kid didn't starve and had a roof over her head was the least you could have done—"

"I want to meet her," his father said on a rush of air, tears welling in his eyes.

Despite his father's obvious contrition, Ryder refused to let his plea derail him, or undermine the resurrected, all-consuming protectiveness that now included Quinn as well as Mel. They came first. As Mel should have then, had Ryder listened to his gut instead of his hormones. Even so, he was curious how far his father's change of heart went.

"Behind Mom's back?"

"If necessary."

Wow. And frankly the idea was at least momentarily tempting, not only for the satisfaction of getting one over on his mother, but because Ryder knew Quinn and his father would get on like gangbusters. However...

"Sorry, Dad, but it's not up to me. Nothing I can do."

"Can't you talk to Mel, feel her out...?"

"She's already made her feelings on the subject more than plain. Hell, if it hadn't been for Quinn's getting hurt she wouldn't even have let *me* meet her."

"But if your mother and I were the ones who set the conditions to begin with—?"

"Conditions you can't simply undo with a wave of your hand because you've changed your mind."

Shoving his trembling hand underneath his glasses, David rubbed his eyelids, then pushed the glasses back into place. "This is torture, Ry, knowing she's so close..." He glanced away, clearly trying to compose himself. "We made a terrible mistake, Ry."

"You think?"

David's gaze met his. "You'll never forgive us for this, will you?"

Anger fisted in Ryder's chest. "Forgive you for what, Dad? For writing off someone you *knew* meant a great deal to me? For rewarding Maureen's loyalty by treating her daughter like trash? For rewarding Jeremy's behavior by absolving him of any responsibility whatsoever—?"

"And if I could undo it, I would! I told you, we—"

"Screwed up. Got it." Ryder got to his feet to dump his unfinished lunch in a nearby garbage can. "But you know what? What I think, whether or not I can forgive you, is immaterial. Because this isn't about either you or me. It's about Quinn. And Mel. Who has no earthly idea what to tell her daughter when she asks about her father—"

"Then let Mel know it's okay to tell Quinn the truth!"

"Here's a better idea—how about *you* let her know that? No, wait—you and Mom. Together. In fact…" Suddenly, he saw the glimmer of a solution, one that kept eluding him as long as he'd kept thinking it was entirely up to him to bring it about. "I'll make a deal with you—you get Mom to admit this was a mistake, and I'll broach the subject with Mel."

Hope bloomed in his father's eyes. "So you'll arrange a meeting?"

"Not so fast. This wound's been festering for way too long to be cleared up by a single 'sorry, we blew it,' so I have no idea what Mel's reaction will be. She might still tell you both to go to hell. And she'd be completely justified."

"Good God, Ry—whose side are you on?"

He pushed out a dry laugh. "The side that would have never let this travesty get as far as it did." At his father's stung expression, Ryder said, more gently, "Dad…I didn't have to come back to St. Mary's, I chose to. Chose to risk Mom's wrath that I didn't become a specialist because I wanted to practice alongside you. Because I feel the work you're doing, right here, is important. And because in many, many ways, I admire the hell out of you. You're the whole reason I became a doctor, okay? So in that respect I will always be on your side."

He laid a hand on his father's shoulder. "But what you and Mom did to Mel was about as far from admirable as it gets. Which you've already admitted. Still, for reasons I've never understood—and don't want to get into now, believe me—you and Mom have each other. Mel…" He shrugged.

His father lifted understanding eyes to his. "You're it."

"Apparently so," Ryder said on a breath as his phone buzzed.

The one-word text was from Mel:

Dinner?

Despite her resolution from the night before, it had taken Mel until after lunch the following day to work up the cojones to text Ryder and take him up on his offer. But she needed to talk to him alone, where Quinn couldn't hear them. And when he texted back, suggesting Emerson's, the town's best seafood restaurant, her mouth watered.

Not that they'd ever been there together, she mused as she parked beside Ryder's sturdy little Toyota RAV in the lot and trudged up the wide plank to the dock bordering the weathered, flat-roofed building—although calling it a building was a stretch—set on pylons in the water. Nobody ever dressed up to go to Emerson's, either, except for the occasional, clueless tourist. Because when you're expected to eat until you pop, you may as well be comfortable. Hence Mel's jeans and faux Uggs now, although she had raised the bar with a dark rose cotton turtleneck and some dangly earrings she'd picked up on a whim at one of the shops in town. Oh, and she'd tossed on some mascara and lipgloss, too. Just for kicks.

Long before she reached the double doors, the scent of steamed crabs and fried fish, spicy crab cakes and hush puppies beckoned, stoking more memories. Inside, the aroma almost made her too dizzy to spot Ryder, seated at one of the oilcloth-covered tables—all the better to crack crabs on—beside a window overlooking the marina and the water beyond.

Shoulder-hugging, dark blue sweater: check. Furrowed brow as he apparently studied the menu he had to have known by heart: check. Huge, delighted smile when he glanced over and noticed her: check.

Hammering heart in reaction to the huge, delighted smile?

Uh-boy.

No sooner had she taken her first nervous steps in his direction, however, than Estelle Emerson, who with her husband Clarence had kept St. Mary's residents', not to mention thousands of tourists', bellies filled for more than thirty years, swooped down on Mel with outstretched arms.

"I don't *believe* it!" she sang out, her dark skin glowing from the steaming pots for the hapless crustaceans that filled those bellies. "Oh, my gracious, girl—aren't you a sight for sore eyes! I remember your daddy and mama coming in here with you when you were a bit of a thing. I heard about your grandma, honey…I'm so sorry. Although I suppose she lived a good long life. You here by yourself?"

"Um, no, actually I'm…" She nodded toward Ryder. One of maybe a half dozen patrons in the place, what with it being off-season. In fact, many of the local joints closed down between September and May altogether. But as Estelle had so often said, what else was she gonna do? Go to Florida for the winter? So she may as well feed whoever was left.

Now Estelle's gaze slid toward Ryder's, then back to Mel. If Estelle knew about their old friendship, Mel had no idea. No reason for her to, she supposed. But her eyes sure lit up now, even as she leaned close to whisper, "You be careful, baby—boy's still nursing a broken heart."

Mel whispered back, "It's okay. So am I."

Now, whatever made her say that, she had no idea. But Estelle's little moan of sympathy, as well as another hug, did feel pretty good, she had to admit. Then the older woman said, her voice even lower, "Just remember—blessings often come out of adversity. You hear?"

"Yes, ma'am," Mel said, polite as she could be, before finally making her way over to the table, blushing when Ryder—all five o'clock shadow and dark, soulful eyes, damn the man—stood to pull out her chair for her. Except Emerson's was not a pulling-out-a-chair kind of place. At least, not before this.

"You look great," he said, sitting back down, and a nervous chuckle burped from Mel's mouth, provoking an understandably curious look from Ryder.

She unwrapped the gigundo paper napkin from around the chintzy flatware. "You don't have to do that."

"Do what?"

"The obligatory 'you look nice' thing. This isn't a date, for heaven's sake."

His brows crashed. Over eyes determined, apparently, to hold hers hostage. Uh-boy, again. "I can't give you a compliment?"

Mel grabbed the Ten Commandments-tablet-sized menu, feeling her cheeks go about the same color as her sweater. Let's hear it for coordination, yay. "It feels... weird, coming from you. I didn't expect it."

"You needed a warning?"

She blubbered out a laugh. "No, I..." Her eyes lowered to the menu. To get away from his, if nothing else. "Just not used to them, that's all."

"From me?"

"From anybody."

His fingers hooked over the top of the menu and yanked it down.

"Hey, I was reading that—"

"You are crazy beautiful," Ryder said. Frowning. "You always have been. I just couldn't say it before."

"But you can say it now."

"Yes. So. What do you want to order?"

You?

Blushing again—this was getting to be a really bad habit, yeesh—Mel cleared her throat as Estelle appeared to take their order. "This," she said, pointing to a combination platter of friend oysters, fried shrimp, fried perch, hush puppies, and Estelle's famous potato salad.

"You want a salad with that?"

As in, iceberg lettuce with some shredded carrots and a tomato wedge.

"Sure. With ranch dressing."

"To keep the arteriosclerosis theme going," Ryder said with a bemused smile after Estelle left.

"Hey. I'd rather shave a few years off my life and die happy than live to a hundred eating cardboard and grass clippings. Although," she said as he chuckled, "if it makes you feel any better I actually love veggies."

"Drenched in butter, I presume."

"Is there any other way?" When he rolled his eyes, she reached over and patted his hand. "I also run and ride a bike. Not to mention cleaning out my grandmother's house is the best cardio workout *ever*. I'm thinking we should charge. But if God hadn't meant for us to eat butter he would've made cows give skim milk. And are we both tap-dancing around why we're really here, or what?"

Ryder leaned back in his chair, one wrist on the edge of the table. "By that, I assume you mean Quinn? Who I assume is with April?"

"No, April's in Richmond. But the Harrises still live next door, and their granddaughter's a year or so older than Quinn, so I pawned her off on them. They were thrilled, she was thrilled, so it was a win-win."

When Ryder chuckled, Mel let her gaze drift outside,

where the sky was turning a deep periwinkle-blue. "But anyway…yes. Quinn."

Who had yet to initiate the "things don't feel right" conversation, even though—as much as the prospect of said conversation freaked her out, because she still had no idea what the heck she was going to tell her—Mel had given the kid several openings throughout the day. So, yeah. Time bomb.

She huffed a sigh, then let her eyes meet Ryder's again, seeing the same compassion that had always been there, but coming from a much deeper place than before. A place of grief and loss that made her ache for him. "My cousins finally knocked some sense into me, that somehow or other I need to lay this issue to rest."

"Really."

"Yep. Like it or not, I can't protect my daughter forever. And she's apparently indicated to April that she can sense that something's off, although she doesn't seem anxious to talk to me about it."

"You think maybe she's afraid of what she'll find out?"

"I have no idea. But she deserves to know who her family is. And it might be better to do this before she hits puberty," she said with a slight smile. "And…I need your help."

After a moment, Ryder leaned forward to slip his hand around hers and her throat went dry. "You got it." Then he released a breath, although not her hand. "Dad wants to meet her. Asked me to arrange a meeting, in fact."

Mel started. "You're kidding?"

"Nope." He gave her hand a brief squeeze before letting go to take a sip of his water. "Not really a surprise, since apparently he was never particularly on board with this, anyway."

"And what did you say?"

Estelle brought them their food; Ryder waited until the steaming, fragrant plates were set in front of them and Estelle was gone, before continuing. "That it was up to you. And that I wouldn't even say anything unless he got Mom to admit *she* screwed up. But since you brought it up first…" He lifted his hands.

Mel dunked a shrimp into a plastic cup of cocktail sauce. "You really think your mother would ever do that?"

"I haven't talked to her since that first night, so I have no idea what she's thinking. But stranger things have happened, I suppose."

"Stranger than your mother actually conceding she was wrong? I doubt it." Fork in hand, Mel tackled the tender, flaky perch, remembering how she'd been the only one of her cousins who actually preferred her fish to taste like fish. Although the things she could do with sole and tilapia had been known to make people weep.

Ryder forked in a bite of his broiled salmon. Weenie. "So how do you feel about letting Quinn and my dad meet?"

"With or without your mother knowing?"

"Either." When Mel hesitated, Ryder leaned forward again. "Honey, there's no way out of this but through it. And maybe if Quinn got to know us—Dad and me, at least—it might diffuse the shock. At least a little?"

For several seconds, Mel stared at her food, twirling her fork in her fingers and wondering why, if she'd already made the decision to move forward, the idea of actually making that move was twisting her up in knots. Finally she lifted her eyes to Ryder's again. "It's just been the two of us for so long. Well, yes, my mother had been part of that, but she's gone, and…" She swallowed. "This is hard—"

"I know it is, sweetheart—"

"No, I mean what I'm about to say." She took a breath, letting it out on a tiny laugh. "Damn, Ry, I am so conflicted about all of this. Sure, finally coming clean about what happened…I know that will be a relief. At least, once the dust settles from the ka-boom. But to be honest, the idea of sharing her isn't sitting all that well."

Ryder's brows pulled together. "You're not going to lose her, Mel."

"No, I know that. Especially since I'm going back to Baltimore as soon as possible. So that's not even an issue, really. But it's more than that. Watching her with Lance— my ex—and then, worse, seeing how torn up she was when it was over…I'm sorry, but your mother is still the unknown quantity in all this. And your father…"

"Is likely to do whatever she wants."

"There is historical precedent."

One side of Ryder's mouth pushed up. "True. So you're concerned Quinn will become attached to my dad and then my mother will find out and put the kibosh on the relationship?"

Mel dunked the next shrimp. Like it'd been accused of witchcraft. "Not only your father."

He frowned, then pushed out a sharp laugh. "Mel, whatever happens, whatever kind of relationship I end up having with Quinn, is up to you. Not my mother. If her opinion didn't sway me then, it sure as hell won't now. If I do become part of Quinn's life," he said carefully, his gaze riveted to hers, "it's for the long haul. Whatever she needs, whatever *you* need, it's yours." Smiling, he raised his hand, three fingers extended. "Scout's honor. *I'm* not going anywhere. Not anymore."

The sincerity in his eyes, his expression… Mel ripped her gaze away from Ryder's to the other diners enjoying their meals, their lives, secure in those lives, while her traitorous heart whispered things that could break that heart, if she let it.

"You don't trust me," he said quietly, and her head snapped back to find something like hurt etched into his features.

"You, I trust. It's all the rest of it…" She shrugged, then let out another little laugh. "I may regret admitting this, but I am *so* tired of doing all the thinking."

"Then lucky for you I'm really, really good at thinking," he said, and she laughed again, and he reached for her hand, again, and that no-account heart started up with the whispering—again—that she'd wasted ten years looking for a clone of what was right in front of her. Especially when he said, "You don't have to do this alone, Mel. I'm right there. Right here, for both you and Quinn. We'll get through this, I promise."

"How?" she squeezed out past the lump in her throat.

"Well…tell you what—Dad and I usually play hooky on Wednesday afternoons, anyway. If the weather cooperates, how about Dad and I take you and Quinn out on the boat for an hour or so? No pressure, just an opportunity for friends to hang out. That way Dad gets to meet her, and, if my hunch is correct, you get an antsy kid out of the house for a little while."

"Oh, Lord," Mel said on a short laugh. "You got that right. Child's about to drive me nuts."

"Then…is it a plan?"

"O…kay. Deal. But I'm gonna need some of that coconut cream pie for fortification."

Grinning, Ryder signaled to Estelle. "Anything for my girl," he said, and Mel seriously considered asking for two pieces.

For the second time in a week, Lorraine's husband had flabbergasted her.

"You're going to do what?"

"Meet our granddaughter," David said mildly as he slipped on his favorite old tennis sweater over a plaid shirt. "Ry thought it might be a good idea for us all to go sailing. And Mel agreed. Reluctantly, though. Can't say I blame her for that."

"Are you saying they've told the child—"

"Quinn."

"They've told…Quinn the truth?"

"Not yet. But that's the plan. At some point."

"And this was Ryder's idea."

"Meeting Quinn?" Tugging down the sweater's sleeves, David shook his head. "Nope. Mine. Now what on earth," he said, vanishing into the walk-in closet, "happened to my deck shoes…?"

"You decided this without even consulting me?"

The found shoes dangling from one hand, David dropped onto the edge of their four-poster bed. "Here's the funny thing, Raney—when I first mentioned to Ry that I wanted to meet Quinn, he said no. Flat out. To protect Mel as well as Quinn, I imagine," he then said, his gaze drifting across the room, as though talking to himself more than Lorraine.

Then his eyes touched hers again, until he dropped them to this shoes, lying on their sides on the thick ivory carpeting, and something about the slump to his shoulders, the more pronounced gray in his hair, made Lorraine suck in a tiny breath. Almost without knowing she was doing it, she braced one hand on the mattress to lower herself to the floor, slip his shoes on his feet. David chuckled.

"What on earth are you doing, Raney?"

"I'm not sure," she said, rapidly tying the first shoelace. "Best not to question it too hard." Then she looked up into the face she loved more than life itself, into the face of the man she knew loved her the same way, even if she often felt she didn't deserve it. "What made him change his mind?" she said, finishing up the second shoelace and awkwardly pushing herself back up to sit beside him, their shoulders touching.

"He didn't. In fact, he first said he wouldn't even consider asking Mel if I could meet Quinn unless I talked to you first. Got you to admit what you—we—did was wrong."

Her face flamed. "I can't do that."

"Of course you could. If you'd just set aside that stubbornness for more than a half second."

She stretched out her hands, blinking at the three-stone diamond ring David had given her for their twenty-fifth anniversary. If only it were that easy. "So why didn't you say something earlier?"

"Because I knew what *you'd* say. And anyway, as it turns out he and Mel had dinner together that very night, and she said she was ready for this all to be over."

Lorraine's stomach clenched. "That's not her decision."

"Yes, Raney," David said, laying a hand on her knee. "It is. Can't protect the kids forever, you know—"

"So, what? You're simply going to rip this whole thing wide open? What about Jeremy? What about *me?*" she said, pressing a hand to her pounding heart.

"What about you?" David said calmly, gently stroking her leg.

"I'll…I'll look like…"

"A fool?"

"David!"

With a final pat to her knee, her husband got to his feet, standing straighter than she'd ever seen him. "It's okay, honey, we can look like fools together. Because for what it's worth—which isn't much at this point, I'll grant you—when the truth does come out, I promise I won't tell

Quinn whose idea it was. That, she doesn't need to know."
He pocketed his keys and cell phone, then cut his eyes to
hers. "I suppose I'd need to clear it with Ryder, first, but...
you could come with us, if you like—"

"What?" She practically jumped to her feet. "No! Are
you *mad?*"

"Clearly. Although you'd only be there as Ryder's
mother, of course. Not Quinn's grandm—"

"I said no! I can't...I couldn't..." Her eyes stinging,
Lorraine walked over to the window overlooking the ex-
panse of lawn interspersed with soaring loblolly pines,
the wharf jutting into the inlet beyond. Her own reflec-
tion stared back at her, pale and distorted. Accusatory. "I
can't," she whispered.

"I understand," David said, dropping a kiss on the top
of her head. Except how could he, when she didn't fully
understand herself?

She whipped around, clutching the front of her sweater.
"So tell me something," she said, her heart hammering
against her knuckles, "if you think what we did was so
wrong, why did you agree to begin with?"

When he turned back, regret flooded his eyes. "Because there would have been hell to pay if I hadn't. Only,
what I didn't realize, was that the debt would still have
to paid, someday. With the kind of interest my stockbro-
ker can only dream about." He ducked his head slightly
to peer at the sun streaming through the pines. "Shaping
up to be a pretty day—the dogs might appreciate a nice,
long walk, hmm?"

His gaze glanced off hers before he walked away.

Chapter Seven

"She'll be fine, Mama," Ryder said as the twenty-foot-long boat, with his father at the helm, smoothly sliced through the cove and out toward the slate-blue, sun-flecked waters of the open bay. "All the times we went out as kids, nobody ever fell overboard."

"You're not just saying that to make me feel better."

Ryder's laugh cut through the motor's whine. "Of course I am. But it's true."

Mel wrenched her gaze from the curly-headed, life-jacketed pumpkin squealing with delight in the seat beside David only to have that gaze slam into the windblown glory that was Ryder. One foot up on the side bench, an arm slung lazily across the back—putting it within scant inches of Mel's shoulder—he was clearly in his element.

And she had to say it made her feel good to see him looking even a little relaxed. Content. She had to resist reaching over, taking his hand. Because that would be entirely inappropriate. Not to mention *stoo*pid.

There'd always been a boat, Mel recalled as she looked away, although David had clearly traded up since the night Ryder had clandestinely taken her out for a short spin when she was thirteen or fourteen—an event that would have frosted *all* their parents had they known. And Mel couldn't deny that the thrum of the motor through her veins, the gentle sting of breeze-blown spray in her face as the sweet little cuddy skimmed the water's surface…fed something inside her as much now as it had on that moonlit night when everything felt possible and it had been enough to simply enjoy that whole big brother-little sister thing they'd had going.

Overhead, an eagle soared, the sun glancing off its white head, its low *kak-kak-kak* competing with the rush of wind in her ears. Spotting it, Quinn pointed.

"Is that an eagle?"

"It is," David shouted. "There's a pair with a nest at the very top of one of the pine trees over there. Watch…"

The magnificent bird dove toward the water, snatching a fish in its talons before flying off again.

"Cool!" Quinn said, and Ryder's father laughed. Quinn hooked a hand over her eyes to watch the bird flap back to its nest. "Mom said the bay's home to lots of birds."

"Yep. More in the warmer months, but still plenty that hang around all year. Or even winter here. You like birds?"

"You kidding?" Quinn said, shoving her more tangled than usual hair behind her ear, where the wind whipped it away again. "I *love* birds…"

"Uh-oh," Ryder said, sliding close enough for Mel to hear him. For his breath to make her skin prickle. "She's got him in the palm of her hand now. Dad took up birding a few years ago, spends nearly every Sunday morning traipsing through marshes and the forests farther inland with binoculars and a guidebook...."

Sure enough, David was grinning to beat the band. "Me, too."

"It's going well, don't you think?" Ryder said, his voice low.

Tensing, Mel glanced away. "That they've bonded like Krazy Glue, you mean?"

"I thought that was the point?"

"I know, I just...sorry," she said, giving her head a sharp shake. "Ambivalence blows. I also keep thinking..." She sucked the inside of her cheek. "How much I wish *my* father was here. That he could have met her." Tears bit at her eyes. "He would've been nuts about her, too."

"I'm sure," he said, then chuckled when Quinn laughed again. "But then, who wouldn't?" He paused. "She's definitely your kid."

Mel smiled. "Does she remind you of me at that age?"

He tilted his head, as though thinking it over. "Some. Not nearly the little pest that you were, though."

"Hah. Wait until you get to know her better."

Too late, she realized what she'd said. Implied. Thankfully Ryder either didn't pick up on her oopsie or decided to take the honorable route and not mention it. "I've got great memories of your father. Seeing him and your mother together, the way they'd kid around...and *fool* around," he said with a grin, and Mel sighed, remembering they'd had no problem with expressing their affection for each other, despite Mom's oft-giggled, "Tony! Not around the children!" "They always seemed so comfortable together."

Mel nodded over the sting at the back of her throat. "I always thought they had the perfect marriage."

"Yeah," Ryder said, his gaze fixed on his father's back six feet away. "Me, too." The rest of that unspoken thought—and Mel had no doubt he'd left things unsaid—trailed out behind them as his father began to circle a grouping of small islands, chatting away to her rapt daughter. "It must've been so hard on your mom, after Tony died."

"It was. He was her rock. Mine, too," she said, then huffed out a breath. "Then I go and get myself knocked up…" Suddenly chilled, she tugged her hood up over her mist-damp, flyaway hair.

"What did she do?" Ryder asked. "After you guys, um, moved?"

Mel allowed a tight smile for Ryder's word choice. "She surprised me, actually. She started her own business, vetting and referring household help for families that still wanted their own domestics rather than using a maid service. It took a while to get it really up and running, of course, but between our survivors' benefits from Social Security and…funds from your parents, we managed. And it gave her something to focus on, keep her mind off things. And once Quinn was born…" She smiled. "She was the best grandmother ever."

"What about yours?"

"Amelia? What about her?"

"She really never spoke to you again?"

"Nope."

"Not even at your mother's funeral?"

"There wasn't one. Mom didn't want anyone to 'make a fuss.' Said, since the family had drifted apart, anyway, what was the point?" She snorted. "Just like Nana, who apparently didn't want a service, either."

"I know."

"Oh, right. Of course," Mel said, thinking that she had no earthly idea what to do with the ashes she'd picked up from the funeral home the day before.

"So I take it she and your mother never patched things up between them, either?"

Mel shook her head. "Not that Mom gave her the chance, since she refused to even tell Nana she was sick. And threatened me within an inch of my life if I did."

Ryder hooked his elbow over the back of the stern, watching the rooster-tail of spray for a moment before saying, "What is it with humans and their damn pride?"

With a short laugh Mel said, "I know, right?" Then she linked her hands over her knees as she watched her daughter, who was clearly having the time of her life. "Why Nana deliberately severed ties with all of us, why we all isolated ourselves from each other, I have no idea. But I'll tell you this—I can't imagine there's anything—*anything*—that Quinn could possibly do that would make me cut her off. Any more than my mother did me, even though I will never, ever forget the look on her face when I told her I was pregnant." Her gaze drifted to Ryder, watching her with a calm intensity that sent a shiver scuttling up her spine. "I'd sliced her heart wide open, and we both knew it."

"Hearts heal," Ryder said. But looking away, as though trying to convince himself of that fact.

"So I hear," Mel said gently, shivering again when he gave her a small smile. "In any case, I don't suppose I'll ever know why Nana never accepted my parents' relationship. Other than the obvious, that she simply didn't think my father was good enough for her daughter. That Mom could have done better." She tucked a stray hank of hair behind her ear. "As if. Hey, cutie-patootie," she said as a grinning Quinn wedged herself between Ryder and Mel with what Mel guessed was a profoundly happy sigh. "Having a good time?"

"Uh-huh," she said with an enthusiastic nod, then twisted to Ryder. "This was the best idea, ever, Ryder!

Thank you! And your dad is so cool! He knows, like, everything about birds and the bay and stuff. He said, if I want, I can go with him the next time he goes birding." She wiggled back around to give Mel the Pleading Hound Dog look. "Can I, Mom?"

Mel's eyes shot to Ryder's, then back to Quinn. "Um, I don't know…we're not going to be here much longer—"

"He said Sunday. That's only a few days from now. So please?"

"We'll see, hon," Mel said, cringing even as the words left her lips. Fortunately, Quinn was too spellbound to call her on the prevarication, instead turning her attention to Ryder, with whom she chattered non-stop the rest of the ride, giggling right on cue in response to his benign teasing.

Just as Mel had done with her father, she realized with a bittersweet pang. And as she listened to their easy, natural interplay, Quinn's sparkling giggles juxtaposed to Ryder's rich laughter, as she caught his delighted glances over her daughter's head—glances that made her heart knock in her chest—she realized she was liking all of this far too much for her own good. For anybody's good.

And yet, as they neared the marina again, she felt like a kid herself, not ready for the outing to end. So when Ryder suggested she and Quinn tag along when he drove out to check on a housebound patient, Mel was hard pressed to find a reason why they couldn't. Shouldn't.

'Course, his smiling right into her eyes and tripping a breaker in her brain might've had something to do with that.

"I've got a better idea," David said to Quinn after they'd disembarked. "You like hot fudge sundaes?"

Quinn's brows dropped. "Dude! Is that a trick question?"

"Not at all," David said, chuckling, as Mel gasped out a mildly horrified, "Quinn! You don't call grown-ups 'dude!'"

Still laughing, David turned to Mel. "Finnegan's decided to stay open year 'round. Thought I'd treat my g—... my new friend while you two go on out to the Washingtons'."

Her stomach jerking at David's slip, Mel reached for her daughter's hand. "Maybe another time, it's kind of cold for ice cream, anyway—"

"No, it's not!" Quinn said, pulling away from Mel to clasp her hands under her chin. Above which her teeth were chattering. "P-please, M-mom?"

"We still have all those cookies at the house. And the cheesecake—"

"And they're all stale and gross!"

"It's only for an hour," David said, his eyes every bit as imploring as her daughter's. Although for completely different reasons, she knew. Reasons that could easily trip him into saying something to Quinn Mel wasn't ready for her daughter to hear. But how was she supposed to do her Mama Bear act with Quinn standing right there? Then Ryder touched her shoulder, making her look up to see that *It's okay, I've got this* look in his eyes before he called to Quinn.

"Hey," he said, holding out his hand to her, "wanna go take a look at that big yacht at the end of the pier?"

Amazingly, she went, although not before lecturing him on how she hadn't held hands with a grown-up since she was six, geez.

After they were a safe distance away, Mel faced Ryder's father again, his yearning expression as he watched Ryder and Quinn mosey on down the dock almost making her wish they didn't have to have this conversation. But before she could speak, he said, "I know. What I almost said." Finally his eyes met hers. "And you have every right to be ticked. And concerned. But I swear it won't happen again."

Mel glanced at her daughter, who was happily yakking poor Ryder's ears off, then back at David. "'Concerned' doesn't even begin to cover it, Dr. Caldwell. 'Worried sick' is more like it, that this whole thing's going to blow up in our faces, that I have no idea how Quinn's going to take this news as it is. At least I'd like to control the when and how." She smiled weakly. "A deluded concept though that might be. Even so," she said on an exhaled breath, "why should I trust you?"

Behind his glasses, self-reproach burned in David's eyes. "Because I already love that little girl with all my heart. I promise you I'd never do anything to hurt her. And the last thing I want to do is get on your bad side."

"A little late for that, isn't it?"

"I know, what we did to you, and her…if you never forgive us for that, I doubt anyone would fault you. Including me. But now that I've met Quinn, I can't imagine not having a relationship of some kind with her. And I daresay neither can Ryder," he said, nodding toward his son and granddaughter walking back toward them, and Mel's breath caught in her throat at Ryder's besotted expression as he watched Quinn zigzag from one side of the dock to the other, still talking a mile a minute. Even a moron could tell how good she'd already been for him.

Or, in her case—big sigh, here—how good *he'd* been for a baggage-ridden chick who'd made "don't trust the bastards" her mantra.

"We only want what's best for Quinn, too," David said quietly. "But how can we prove that if you don't give us a chance?"

She met the older man's gaze. "And Mrs. Caldwell? Is she included in that 'us'?"

"Right now she's all wound up in that damn pride of hers," he said, and Mel thought of Ryder's earlier comment. "It's hard for her…" Clearing his throat, he glanced down, then lifted sheened eyes to Mel. "To admit she made a mistake. Or to ask for forgiveness. Doesn't mean she's not thinking about it, though. Thinking about it hard, too, if you ask me. Mel," he said when she turned away. "There are certain…things you don't know."

Her head snapped back around. "What things?"

"Things I'm not at liberty to discuss at present. All I can say is, there might have been more behind Lorraine's actions than appeared on the surface. Not that she said anything directly, but I know my wife. And right now, I know she's struggling."

As Mel gaped at David, a red-cheeked Quinn bounded up to them. Followed by an ambling Ryder, hands in pockets, his relaxed smile at odds with the obvious longing in his eyes. Eyes which connected with hers, rife with undefined questions.

"So did you decide?" Quinn said, grabbing Mel's hand. "If I can go get ice cream with Dr. David?"

No mean feat, making a decision when your brain cells were in roller derby mode, slamming against the inside of your skull, taking each other out, *splat!* But a decision she made, based on two things: one, that she truly believed David wouldn't spill the beans, if for no other reason than she doubted he'd want to deal with the fallout by himself; and two, that letting Quinn hang out with Ryder's father gave Mel the perfect opportunity to grill Ryder about his mother.

"How long do you think we'll be?" she asked Ryder.

"Hour, hour and a half—"

"Take your time," David said, smiling down at Quinn. "We're in no hurry. Are we, Quinn?"

Then two sets of eyes canted to Mel's. Sheesh.

"Oh, all right," she said, and Quinn gave Mel a hard hug before falling in step beside David, chattering away and matching him stride for stride as they marched down the dock and into what Mel suddenly realized was her future.

Like it or not.

Ten minutes later, after she'd taken advantage of the marina's facilities to "freshen up," as Nana used to say, they were whizzing past vast, flat fields of just-harvested farmland and Ryder had once again fallen into pensive mode. Not somber, she didn't think, but definitely contemplative. Not unheard of even when he'd been a teenager. Although then, according to her mother when Mel had complained about his crazy mood swings, he'd been at the mercy of some vicious hormones. Now he had cause—

"I know that wasn't easy," he said, making her flinch. "Leaving Quinn with Dad."

"There's an understatement," she grumbled.

"I'd say it's going to be okay, but I don't want to get smacked."

"Good call."

He chuckled. Good to know she hadn't lost her touch. Except he sank into silence again, making Mel think maybe this wasn't the best time to get chit-chatty about his mother. So instead she said, "Where are we going again?"

"You remember old Moses Washington? Used to have a fruit-and-vegetable stand out on the highway—"

"Where Mom used to take us?" *All* of them, Mel thought with a half smile—Blythe and April as well as Ryder, piled like puppies in her parents' Dodge Caravan, wearing flip-flops and terrycloth coverups and smelling of sunscreen and cherry Popsicles. "You bet." Then she frowned. "Is he sick?"

"Just old, mostly. Turned eighty last month."

"Get *out*. Really? Wow."

"Yeah. His heart's not what it used to be. Or his mind, unfortunately. Which is why I go out there, since bringing him into the clinic confuses him. He still lives in his house, but his oldest daughter Nina and her husband live with him now, since his wife died five, six years ago." He flashed her a grin. "Fair warning—there will undoubtedly be pie of some kind. Which Nina will expect you to eat."

"I can do that," Mel said, then laughed. "Gosh, it seems like a million years ago. Those summers." She blew another, shorter laugh through her nose. "How on earth— *why* on earth—did you put up with three teenyboppers like that? The giggling alone must've driven you insane."

"Speaking of understatements."

"Then—"

"I don't know, really. I never really thought about it. I guess because those outings…they were fun. You guys were fun. *And* you let me boss you around."

Mel sucked in a shocked breath and gently swatted his shoulder. "We did not! Take it back!"

"Hey," Ryder said, laughing, "cut it out, I'm driving! And I did, too, boss you guys. And you *loved* it."

"You are *so* dead," she said without thinking, only to mentally swat herself when his smile faded. "Sorry, sorry, sorry…God, what an idiot—"

"You are many things, Mel," Ryder said in a very low voice, "but you are not, and never have been, an idiot." His eyes bounced to hers, then away. "Is that clear?"

Unable to speak, she could only nod.

Then they rounded a bend in the road, startling a small flock of Canada geese into flight against the hazy blue sky. Ryder's gaze followed for a moment, his expression tense when he returned his attention to the road. And Mel thought, *Ah*.

"It takes a long, long time," she said at last, "before you stop feeling like there's a blunt instrument lodged inside your chest. Before everything stops reminding you of them."

A faint smile stretched his lips. "Dang. You're good."

"Familiar territory. I'd recognize it blindfolded."

Another two, three fields zipped past before he said, "For what it's worth, the constant pain faded months ago. But it still has a nasty way of blindsiding me when I least expect it. The geese…Deanna loved them. Noisy, obnoxious birds with no sense of personal space whatsoever, barely one step above pigeons as far as I'm concerned, but…" Smiling, he shook his head, then blinked, too quickly. "We wanted three kids. One of each, she used to joke."

"Sounds like my kind of gal."

"I think you would have liked her very much. She was very down-to-earth, despite—"

When he stopped, Mel's eyebrows lifted. "Despite what? Oh. Being pedigreed, you mean?" She scratched the side of her neck. "Bet your mother adored her."

"Although I had no idea when we met," he said, and Mel didn't miss that he'd sidestepped her last comment. "She did a lot of volunteer work with wildlife conservation in the area. One of the other volunteers got hurt one day, and she brought him to the clinic, the pair of them wet and filthy and smelling like the marsh."

"And you fell like a ton of bricks."

"Something like that."

Mel laughed, picturing Ryder getting emotionally sideswiped by this mud-drenched goddess reeking of rotten eggs. "I take it she cleaned up okay?"

"Yes," he said after a moment. "She did."

Mel's eyes filled. "I'm so sorry, Ry."

"Thanks."

Several more seconds passed before she said, "And you really haven't dated since?"

"No. Oh, once or twice my mother foisted someone on me and I took her out to dinner, but I'm sure I would have won a Worst Date award. Even though intellectually I know I need to move on."

"Meaning your parents are pressuring you to."

"No. Well, maybe a little."

"Hey." She poked one finger into his arm. "You'll know when the time's right. And nobody can know that *except* you. So don't you let anybody bully you into something you're not ready for, you hear me?"

"Yes, ma'am," he said, his grin coming out from hiding.

"And in the meantime…you can be as much of an uncle to Quinn as you want."

His eyes cut to hers. "You sure?"

"Yes."

"I'd like that. But…" He paused. "I can only accept if you're part of the package."

Mel started. "I…? What?"

"I'd forgotten how easy it is to talk to you. I know, I know—we can't go back to what we had. And I don't want to." He glanced at her, then away. "But what we've got now…well. I like it. And I'd like to keep it. If that's okay with you."

"Even long distance?" she said softly.

"Whatever works for you. And Quinn."

Sighing, Mel faced front. "I suppose that depends on all the other stuff. And according to your father," she said, figuring she might as well go for it, "there's apparently more 'stuff' than I'd at first realized."

"Like…what?"

"Not sure. Since all he said was, that there were 'things'—" she made air quotes "—he wasn't at liberty to discuss. About your mother."

His voice lowered. "Really?"

"Yeah. Got any idea what he's talking about?"

"None." Ryder flexed his hands on the wheel. "Although I suppose you want me to find out."

"Oh, right. And how exactly do you propose to do that?"

"Ask her?"

Mel laughed. "This is your mother we're talking about—"

"Mel. As insane as this all is, it's also the first thing in nearly a year that's made me focus on something besides myself. And I'll do anything in my power to make this right. You have my word."

It'd been so long since she'd felt as though someone was truly and completely on her side. Not since she'd been a kid, in fact, and she'd known she could trust Ryder with her life. As far as that went, he was right—nothing had changed, even if both of them had. But as she said, "Thanks," and he nodded, determination sharpening a jaw that didn't need any more definition, she felt a wave of something trickle through her that she sure as hell hoped was gratitude.

Because anything else would be disastrous.

"So I take it you had a good time?"

Bouncing a little in the slippery red booth after the waitress took their order, Quinn nodded for Dr. David, even though her head felt like it was about to explode from all the questions inside it. 'Cause you better believe, after what she'd overhead? She'd been watching her mom and Ryder's dad *real* closely. Especially when Ryder had taken her away so Mom and Dr. David could talk—like *that* wasn't obvious, geez—Quinn had kept sneaking peeks at them. Not that she could tell anything, although Mom had seemed kind of nervous, maybe. But then Mom had let Quinn go with Ryder's dad, right? So how bad could it—whatever "it" was—be?

"On the boat, you mean? Yeah, it was cool."

"Good," Ryder's dad said with a smile as he dug his phone out of a pocket over his chest, texting something before putting it away again. "Thought you might like it."

"Mom'll probably make me write a report, though," she said, making a face, and he laughed, sounding a lot like Ryder.

"Ry tells me your mother homeschools you."

And why she couldn't just do what April said, and tell Mom what she was feeling, she didn't know. But it was like the words would get stuck in her throat or something. Like she wanted to know what was going on, yeah, but she was also scared of what she might find out. And besides, it wasn't like there was any guarantee Mom would tell her the truth, anyway, right?

"Yeah. Since I was four."

"Have you ever been to regular school?"

"Once. When I was in the second grade. Because Mom thought maybe I was missing out by not being around other kids."

"Were you?"

She shrugged. "Not really. For one thing, I like being by myself—at least sometimes—and for another I was already so far ahead of everybody else that I kept saying stuff that made them mad. Not on purpose, I don't mean that. But like I'd be all surprised when they didn't know how to do something I'd known for a year already. Not the best way to make friends," she said on a sigh. "And anyway, I was bored to *tears,* and the teacher didn't really know what to do with me, so Mom asked me what I wanted to do and I said I wanted to go back to being homeschooled."

Dr. David's phone buzzed; he pulled it out, checked the message, then set it on the table in front of him just as the waitress brought them their ice cream. Wow. That was a lot of whipped cream. Not that this was a problem.

"What's your favorite part about being homeschooled?"

Quinn picked up her spoon and dug in. "Not having to get up early," she said, and Dr. David laughed again. "And staying in my pj's, if I want. Sometimes Mom does, too. Because that's how we roll. This," she said, jabbing the spoon toward the ice cream, "is seriously excellent."

"It is that—"

"Can I ask you something?"

Dr. David gave her one of those oh-heck-now-what looks like she'd seen on Mom's face a gazillion times. "Sure."

And to be honest, for a second Quinn thought about asking him straight out about what she'd overheard. Only, for one thing, she wasn't really sure what to ask. Or how. And for another, whatever it was, she was pretty sure she needed to hear it from Mom. But there was this one question about to burn a hole in her brain, and she figured if anybody could answer it, it would be Ryder's dad.

"Mom says she and Ryder were friends when they were kids."

"They were. Very good friends."

"Like, best friends?"

The doctor rubbed a knuckle over his chin. "I think Ryder thought of your mother like a little sister. It made him feel good, having her to look out for. Take care of."

"Oh. He didn't have any brothers or sisters of his own?"

Dr. David went real still, except for twisting his spoon around and around over his sundae. Hot fudge, like hers. "Actually, he does. A younger brother. Jeremy."

"So how come he didn't play with him? Instead of my mother?"

The doctor's eyes bounced to hers, then back to his ice cream. And there it was again. That weird feeling. Like she was playing the hot-cold game with the truth, and she was getting really warm.

"They had—have—very different personalities. They never did get along particularly well. That happens some-times. In families."

Quinn spooned a gooey spoonful of ice cream into her mouth, barely catching the runny fudge before it dripped all over her chin. "So what you're saying is," she said around the coldness, "Ryder liked my mother better than his own brother?"

The doctor's mouth moved, like he couldn't decide whether to smile or not. "In many ways, yes. I suppose he did." Now he frowned. "Is that what you wanted to ask me?"

"What? Oh, no. Sorry. I guess I got off track. Mom is always on my case about that, she said if I'd ever actually finish the conversation I started she'd fall over in a dead faint. But anyway, that couldn't've been my question, any-way, right? Since I didn't even know Ryder had a brother. Does he live here?"

"No. In New York. We don't see him much."

"How come?"

"Just living different lives, I suppose."

"That is so sad. I mean, maybe because it's only Mom and me, since my grandmother died, but I think it would be so cool to have more family. *Anyway,* sorry, I did it again—my question *is*…do you think Ryder and my mom maybe like each other more than just friends?"

The doctor half coughed, half laughed. "And there's a question I don't dare answer, because no matter what I say I'm bound to get in trouble." He looked up as the door jangled open behind her, then back at Quinn. "But how would you feel if they were?"

"Me? I think that'd be the coolest thing ever," she said on a sigh, mushing her ice cream so the fudge sauce got all mixed in. "And since they're friends already, it sorta feels like a no-brainer, if you ask me. That they'd get together." She grinned. "And then I could stay here and you and I could go do all that cool birding stuff, huh?"

For the first time, Dr. David's face relaxed. "That would be nice. Very nice." Smiling, he lifted his glass of water, like Mom would do with the sparkling cider on holidays. So Quinn picked hers up and toasted him back as he said, "Here's to everybody's dreams coming true."

Giggling, Quinn clinked glasses with him, then concentrated on what was left of her sundae, on feeling *good,* for once, good enough that the spooky feeling was almost gone.

Although the questions? They weren't going anywhere.

Lorraine doubted Quinn had seen David's glance over her head when the child refocused on her sundae, her gingery curls bobbing in time with her swinging feet. Just as she clearly hadn't seen the brief flicker of surprise in David's eyes when she came in, lifting a finger to her lips before sliding into a booth far enough away to not be seen, but close enough to observe. To listen.

He probably didn't know what to make of it, since low key had never been her style. After all, what was the point in arriving someplace if people didn't *know?* Not this time, however. Goodness, she'd even dressed in all beige, as though to become as invisible as possible.

All the better to get her heart shredded, she supposed. Even more than it already was.

Truth be told, when David had first texted her, telling her where they were, giving her the opportunity to change her mind, she'd texted back, *No way.* Except curiosity nagged at her until finally it melted the fear. Or at least softened it enough to push past it. So here she was, shredded heart and all, observing her grandchild—the bright, funny, forthright grandchild who reminded Lorraine so much of herself she could barely take it in—she'd sworn never to lay eyes on. The child she'd tried so hard to forget.

Except she hadn't. Not even for a moment.

The waitress came; Lorraine ordered coffee, even as she found herself giving grudging props to Melanie for raising the girl on her own. How well she'd obviously done, how she'd clearly refrained from contaminating the child with what had to have been her own asperity about…circumstances.

Remorse battering her psyche like hurricane-churned surf at a seawall, Lorraine slowly pressed a fist to her chest as her soul cried out for the child, images flashing of shopping trips to New York, of debutante and engagement parties, of a lavish, early summer wedding in their backyard…

All fantasy, of course, she thought with a rude thud as she crashed back to earth. Because it was too late, wasn't it—?

She sucked in a little breath.

Honestly, the answer was so obvious, so simple, she couldn't believe it had taken this long for it to come to her. Although she didn't suppose that, relatively speaking, it had taken so long at that. Especially since, once it did, the plan practically exploded in her thought, full-blown.

And with the plan came peace. A sense of having regained her footing, of once more being in control. Because for as long as she could remember, it had always been about The Plan. Naturally The Plan changed according to the needs of the moment, but Lorraine had never been someone given to simply "letting" things happen. That was pure foolishness, as far as she was concerned.

But at least this plan, she mused when the coffee arrived and she removed a couple dollars from her purse to pay for something she had no intention of drinking, should not only make everyone happy, for once, but—and here was the best part—as far as she could tell had already been put into motion years before.

And not by her.

Amazed by her own brilliance, Lorraine dropped the bills on the table, blew a kiss to her husband, and slipped out as unobtrusively as she'd arrived.

Kiss her.

Kissherkissherkissherkissherkissher....

Yeah, it'd been pretty much like that for the past hour or so. Why, Ryder had no idea. Okay, not entirely true. Considering how firmly Mel had been kicking his grief in the butt all afternoon he probably wanted to kiss her out of sheer gratitude, if nothing else.

Which wasn't entirely true, either.

They'd finished up with Moses and were headed back to town. How the old man had recognized her when he rarely recognized Ryder anymore was a mystery in itself. But damned if his bleary, yellowing eyes hadn't lit up when, smiling, Mel had leaned over to give him a hug, then squatted at his knees, tightly holding his gnarled, trembling hand while he rambled on piecemeal about things that had happened years ago...

"Feels like another storm's coming in. The temperature's dropped," she said beside him, hugging herself.

Underneath her breasts.

Fine. He was horny. And lonely. And so bleeping tired of being miserable. And lonely. And horny. And Mel was funny and sexy without even trying, and underneath her grumpiness had a heart as big as her boobs—bigger—and made him laugh, dammit, and how long had it been since he'd laughed without feeling like he was playing the part of a man who was coping just fine, thank you?

"Yeah, looks like," he said, peering up at the glowering sky and away from Mel's...attributes.

But the thing was, wanting to kiss Mel didn't mean he still didn't miss Deanna. Or that being around Mel obliterated the pain, even if it had seemed to recede a bit more than usual. Like the tide.

Which always returned, didn't it?

Then she sighed, making the breasts rise like warm dough—no way to miss it without looking completely to his left—and Ryder thought, *I am a terrible, terrible person.*

A chill rippled through the car; Ryder reached out to punch on the heat. "You warm enough?"

"Me? Yeah, this fleece stuff is warmer than it looks. How about yourself?"

He grimaced at the windbreaker that had seemed more than adequate that morning. "Freezing. In fact, do you mind if we stop by my house so I can grab another jacket? It's on the way."

"'Course not."

"You sure? I know you want get back to Quinn."

Silence reverberated between them for a moment before she said, "It's okay. *I'm* okay." She laughed a little. "And I'm sure Quinn's more than okay. Although your dad's brain cells might be slightly crispy around the edges by now."

"Can't imagine who she gets the chatty gene from," Ryder said, grinning, feeling almost...okay. Normal. Even when Mel squawked.

Especially when Mel squawked.

A few minutes later he pulled up in front of the smallish, gabled concoction he and Deanna had bought two years ago, wondering when—if—the time would ever come that he could look at the house and not feel the pang of unrealized dreams. Mel angled her head to study the place for several seconds before slowly nodding.

"I like it," she said. "It's very 'you.'"

Us. It was supposed to have been very us.

He pushed open his car door. "I'll only be a sec, you can stay here—"

"Like hell," she said, getting out and starting up the flagstone path toward the hundred-year-old, beige-and-white two-story house, the soft denim of her jeans perfectly molding to her shapely bottom, and lust flared. *Whoosh.*

Embrace the horniness, the voice said inside him, and he literally bit his cheek to staunch the thought. Except...

What was, was.

"It's a work in progress," Ryder said, catching up. "I'm doing a lot of the renovation myself and I only have nights and weekends."

"Then I'm even more impressed," Mel said as he reached around her to unlock the front door, catching another whiff of the scent that had been driving him crazy for hours, and his gut cramped again, from longing, from grief, from the guilt slicing him to shreds.

But instead of moving out of his way Mel looked up at him, her eyes soft with understanding, her mouth tilted. A full mouth. Some might even call it luscious, all dewy with the pink lipgloss she'd smeared on in the car after they'd left Moses.

Kill. Him. Now.

"As I recall," she said, "you barely passed woodshop in middle school."

He pushed the door open. "You remember that?"

"It's downright scary, the vast assortment of useless crap stuffed in my brain," she said, stepping inside. "It's worse than my grandmother's house in there…ohhh, nice." She unzipped her fleece hoodie, making herself—and her breasts, and her shiny mouth—right at home. Hips swaying, she crossed to the brick fireplace over freshly varnished oak floors, skimming her fingers over the matching, refinished wood mantel. "Wow. This is *gorgeous*. You stripped it yourself?"

"All twelve coats. And yes, it was hell, thanks for asking."

She chuckled, then slid her hands into her back pockets, lifting her eyes to take in the dove-gray walls, the trio of white-paned windows along the back overlooking a serene, duck-infested tidewater marsh in the distance—the house's main selling point, according to Deanna, Ryder thought on another pang.

"You bought this for her, didn't you?" Mel said, and Ryder's pulse tripped.

"We bought it together, yes."

"And yet, you kept it."

"Yeah," he breathed out. "Although I can't tell you how many times I came this close—" he lifted his hand, thumb and forefinger pinched together "—to listing it. How long it took before I could even set foot in the place without…." He shook his head, his throat closing up.

"I'm sure," Mel said, so much tenderness in her voice, and Ryder thought he would expire from wanting to press close all that warmth and generosity. "And you used the reno as therapy, right?"

"Something like that. Figured I should have something more to show for it than a pile of canceled checks."

She gave him a thumbs-up, then inspected the white wainscoting it'd taken him hours to get right. "After my father died, my mother launched herself into I don't know how many 'projects,' anything and everything to keep her distracted. And when we moved to Baltimore it only got worse, when she finally had a place of her own to decorate however she chose. How much of the house is done?"

"Just downstairs. And…the master bedroom."

She turned, giving him that inscrutable look. "It still hurts, doesn't it?"

"Dammit—how do you do that? Read my mind?"

"Read your face, you mean? Seriously, Ry, it's a fabulous house, but…if it's causing you this much anguish maybe you *should* ditch it. Not that this has anything to do with me—"

"More than you might think," he said, releasing another breath when her eyebrows lifted. "When the sheriff came to my door that night…it was like something broke inside me. Yes, I'm mending, but a lot more slowly than I'd ever imagined. But at least I'd actually gotten to the point where I could walk through the front door and not hear Deanna's voice, or imagine her looking out the window, or sitting on the floor with a bunch of paint samples spread out in front of her. But then, today, being with Quinn…"

He finally grabbed his canvas coat off the rack by the front door. "All those conversations Dee and I had, about having kids…the plans we had… Crap, I hate sounding like this." A short, sharp laugh escaped from his throat. "*Feeling* like this."

Mel took a couple of steps closer. "And who's to say you won't fall in love again? Get married, have those kids—"

"Mel, stop. Please."

"Sorry," she muttered, rezipping her own jacket, jerking when his hand closed around her arm.

"No, you don't understand…" But then, how could she, when he didn't, either?

Ryder sank onto the Shaker bench by the front door, the one they'd found at some flea market or other, his head in his hands. Where it still was when he sensed Mel kneel in front of him, just as she had with Moses. After a moment she reached up and tugged his hands away from his face, her earnest, perplexed expression threatening to rip him in two.

"Hey. Talk to me."

"You've got to get back—"

"Not immediately. What's going on?"

"I can't—"

"Don't even give me that. If you can't be honest with me, then who?"

A raw laugh scraped his dry throat before he met her gaze. "It would appear I have the hots for you so badly I can barely think straight."

And with that, Mel's hormones exploded into flight like a bunch of hyper, hungry, woefully confused moths. Then she burst into laughter.

"You brought me here to have your wicked way with me?"

"*No!* God, no! Why would you even think that? And stop laughing!"

"Ohmigod, Ryder, you're beet-red!"

"It's not funny, Mel!"

"Sorry, Mr. I'm-always-in-control. It's freaking hysterical!"

His gaze bored into hers. "I did not bring you here to have sex with you."

"But you sure as heck thought about it."

After a second or two, he groaned again, then collapsed against the wall behind the bench, his fingertips pressed into his eyelids. "Only about five hundred times."

"Wow."

His hands dropped to his lap. "You really had no clue?"

"None. Then again, I wasn't exactly looking for clues, either. I mean, after our conversation in my grandmother's kitchen, I thought…well. That it was sort of a non-issue?"

"I said I found you appealing."

"*And* that you had no intention of acting on it. So, uh, I take it things have changed?"

His mouth clamped shut, Ryder pushed a long, shaky breath through his nose. "I'm so sorry."

"For being human? Please." He grunted. "Poor baby. How long has it been?"

"Long enough for me to act stupid, apparently."

"*Thinking* is not acting, Ry."

"Not much difference in my book."

Still on her knees, Mel rested her folded arms across his thighs. Thought really, really hard about where to take this. If anywhere. Because either this was an unexpected opportunity she'd kick herself for if she let it go, or a temptation she'd kick herself for if she didn't. No way of telling.

"So what you're saying is, the numbness has worn off. And now everything's…" She fought a smile and lost. "Prickling."

"Not helping, Mel."

"But…" *What the hell, right?* "I…could."

On what sounded like a tortured laugh, Ryder finally

curled forward, capturing her hands in his to tuck against his chest. "Except that would be…" My goodness, *such* a big sigh. "Beyond wrong."

"Depends how you define 'wrong'."

"Mel, I'm—"

"Still mourning Deanna. Got it. No, I swear. I know exactly what this is. Or, more to the point, it isn't. And…oh, for crying out loud—"

Without further ado Mel shifted, gripped his shoulders and laid one on him.

Or tried to.

Clearly startled, Ryder reared back. Frowning. "What are you doing?"

"It's called kissing. Strike a chord, maybe?"

"But—"

"Ryder. One—you know you want to, and two—good news! I'm not sixteen anymore."

"But…" He frowned even harder. She considered telling him his face was going to freeze like that. "But it's *you*."

"Yeah, it's me. Who you just admitted to lusting after, oh, ten seconds ago? And more good news!" She flung out her arms. "I'm okay with that. So pucker up, buster. And if it *does* feel bizarre—because I suppose that's always a possibility, although frankly I'd be surprised—then we'll know and you can stop tormenting yourself." She skootched closer on her knees. "Ready?"

The trembly smile only marginally mitigated the horror in his eyes. "You're insane."

"Goes without saying." She tapped her mouth. "Lips. Here. *Now*—"

The last word was swallowed up—pretty much literally—when he finally booted those pesky qualms and planted one on her for the history books.

Wow. Pent-up volcanoes had nothing on this guy.

And yes, it was everything she could have wished for. And more. All that fantasizing as a kid, about what his mouth would feel like pressed to hers, didn't even begin to compare to the mind-blowing reality. Lordamercy, those poor moths didn't know what to do with themselves.

And yet, Mel mused, shortly after he'd lowered her to the hooked rug in the entry way and their tongues had become intimately acquainted, and despite his pounding heartbeat underneath her palm, we weren't talking wild and wooly, either. Oh, no, homeboy knew exactly what he was doing. And since Mel did, too…well, this was the most fun she'd had in months.

And all they were doing was making out.

For now, she thought with a mental eyebrow waggle as his hand wandered close enough to the outside of one breast to make her hoo-hah quiver in hope. And it was more than evident that she had his *full* attention.

Finally Ryder lifted his head and frowned into her eyes. Mel frowned back. *"What?"*

"It wasn't bizarre."

"Damn me with faint praise, why not?"

Finally the frown eased. A little. "Actually…I liked it. A lot."

"Yeah? Me, too. You kiss good, Caldwell. *Real* good."

That merited a slight grin. Along with—still—no small amount of uncertainty around the eyes, but she'd take whatever she could get. "You, too."

Palming her stomach, Mel propped the back of her head in her other hand. "So you wanna fool around or what?"

He sighed. "I don't know."

"Oh, but I think you do."

"It's not that easy, Mel."

"Only because you're making it complicated. Ryder," she said when he looked away. "I think it's pretty obvious we both need an outlet. Desperately, if that smooching session was anything to go by. So that's all this is. Or will be. Friends helping each other out."

Slowly, his eyes swung back to hers. "This from the woman who a week ago wasn't even sure if she wanted to have dinner with me."

"What can I tell you, things change."

Again with the intense gaze. "You could really put all the other stuff aside?"

"You mean, the family issues? First off, none of that is between us. It never was. Second, it's not often I get to do something just for myself. And I'm guessing you don't, either. So this is for us, okay? Has nothing to do with anyone else. And so help me, if you even *think* of saying you're afraid of hurting me, I will smack you. You don't have to protect me anymore, *capice?*"

Then she reached up to skim a fingertip down that lovely, scratchy, oh-so-male cheek, and his eyes darkened, making her shiver so hard she nearly fell apart right there and then. Pitiful. "S-so. You good to go?"

Blowing a soft laugh through his nose, Ryder grabbed her hand to press a kiss into her palm—uh, yeah, more shivering—then arched one eyebrow. "In fifteen minutes?"

"Right now, sweetcheeks? I'd be good with five."

Laughing softly, Ryder got to his feet and hauled her to his.

And did not lead her upstairs.

"You are so dead," she muttered, only then he took her face in his hands and kissed her again—a nice, long, deep one, too—confusing the hell out of her.

"What—?"

"I need to think about this, for one thing. And for another, I can't do that to you."

"Oh, honey, you can do anything you like—"

"No, I mean…" Somehow he managed to chuckle and sigh at the same time. Talented. "Do you cut corners when you're making one of your fancy dishes?"

"Depends on how much of a hurry I'm in. Because sometimes good enough is, well, good enough."

So what does the turkey do? Wrap her up all nice and close against that warm, solid, soapy-scented chest. Honestly. "You're not making this any easier."

"Neither are you, buster."

He let her go to scoop his coat off the floor where it had landed somewhere along the way, then hunched into it. "And maybe I think you deserve more than 'good enough.' Even though…" He shook his head, then opened the door for her. Frowning.

With an award-worthy eyeroll, Mel plopped her wrists on his shoulders. "Even though this would only be about stress relief. Well, lemme tell you something, bub—if you make love half as well as you kiss, I will count myself one of the luckiest women on the planet. Get it?"

Then—hallelujah!—the doofus smiled. "I think this is what's called a paradigm shift."

"Heck, yeah," Mel said, and kissed him again, and moths went wild.

Normally Quinn was okay with helping Mom make dinner. But after two rainy days where there'd been nothing to do except school stuff and help Mom clean out stinky closets, when the sun finally did appear she was so antsy Mom told her to go outside, for heaven's sake, before she drove her and April—who'd gotten back from Richmond that morning—nuts. Now, sitting with her legs dangling over the edge of the still wet dock behind the house, Quinn squinted against the bright orange rays of the setting sun as the wind gripped her neck, making her shiver.

There he was again.

He was standing on the shore, with the dog, close enough to get a halfway decent look. She'd seen him maybe twice more after that first time, but always from the window or back porch, too far away to talk to. Now she could see he was older than she'd first thought. Taller, too.

He was also looking straight at her, the sun turning his light hair a weird pumpkin color.

"You live here now?" he called out.

"No, just visiting," Quinn yelled back, although she wished that weren't true. The little town with all the really old houses and shops and stuff, and being able to see so much sky, and the way the water changed colors…she felt like she belonged here. And she didn't care what was or wasn't going on between her mom and Ryder's parents; she really liked Ryder's dad, too. Then she remembered the boy. "You can come out here and talk to me, if you want. So we don't have to keep yelling at each other."

So he did, to sit cross-legged on the dock with the dog between them—who was big and black and smelly and kept trying to lick Quinn's face, making her laugh.

"Bear! No! Sit!" The boy grabbed the dog's collar, shoving his butt down to the wood. "Sit!" He sat, sorta, but like he had electricity going through him, his tiny yellow eyes fixed on Quinn as he about wiggled out of his glossy black fur.

Finally the dog calmed down, at least enough for them to introduce themselves. The boy's name was Jack, he said, he was eleven and went to the Friends' school in town, and he lived five houses away—he pointed to a big, blue house with a smaller boat than Ryder's dad's, docked at its own marina—but his father was in congress, so he lived part-time in Washington.

"What about your mom?"

A couple seconds passed before Jack said as he petted the dog, "She died. A year ago. So it's just me and Dad. Well, and my grandparents. What happened to your hand?"

"What? Oh." Quinn glanced at the stitches, which itched something awful but Ryder said they had to stay in for two weeks. "I cut myself on a nail. It doesn't hurt or anything."

"Can I see?"

"Sure."

She stuck out her hand; Jack stared at the wound for a couple of seconds, then nodded. "So are you here with your parents?"

"My mom, yeah. I don't have a dad. In fact, I don't even know who he is."

"Really?" His hand went still in the dog's fur. "You mean, like your mother went to a sperm bank or something?"

Quinn frowned. "What's that?"

"You really don't know?" When she shook her head, he lifted his chin, like he thought he was hot stuff for knowing something she didn't. "It's this place where women go if they wanna have a baby but don't have a husband. There's these two kids in school, their mom did that. So they don't know who their dad is, either."

"Huh." Quinn thought a moment. "I don't know, but maybe. I'll have to ask her." Although if that was true, why didn't Mom simply say that? Honestly.

They were both quiet for a moment before Jack said, "It sucks, not having my mom anymore," and Quinn felt all squirmy inside, although she didn't know why.

"I bet it does. I mean, I never knew my dad, so I can't miss him, but my mom…I can't imagine…" She couldn't even finish the thought, it made her so sad. "I'm sorry. For you, I mean." And she was, even if he did act like a know-it-all. Jack shrugged, and Quinn decided they needed to get off this subject. "Do you know Dr. Caldwell?"

He gave her a funny look. "Which one? The old one or the young one?"

"Young."

Frowning, he picked up a stick that'd blown onto the dock and tossed it into the water and the dog jumped in after it. "Yeah. Why?"

"I think maybe my mother likes him. You know, like a boyfriend."

Jack's eyebrows got all bunched up. "Why are you telling me this?"

Quinn's face got all hot. Because he had a point—why on earth *was* she talking about this? Especially to a complete stranger? Ohmigosh, Mom would *kill* her.

"I don't know. Forget it, it was stupid—"

"Does he like her back?"

She turned to see Jack looking at her with this real strange expression. Huh. "I don't know," Quinn said, sighing. "It's not like anybody tells me anything."

"Tell me about it." The stick clamped in his jaws, Bear swam toward the shore, climbed out, shook, then trotted back to lay the dripping stick on Jack's lap. Jack threw it again, then curled his hands around the edge of the pier, watching the dog. "Dr. Ryder was supposed to marry my cousin."

Quinn's jaw nearly dropped off. Holy cannoli. "You're kidding? What happened?"

"She died. In…in the same car crash that killed my mother."

"Ohmigosh…" Feeling totally dumb and helpless, but mostly dumb, that she'd wanted to change the subject only she'd managed to bring it right back again, Quinn looked out over the water, shivering. Then, not knowing why, she reached for Jack's hand. His head jerked around, looking all shocked and stuff, but he didn't let go. At least not right away. And when he did, to throw the stick *again,* he said, "Um…you wanna come to my house sometime and play Mario Kart?"

"Sure. Okay," she said, and he gave her a shy grin, making her feel like maybe she wasn't so dumb, after all.

And what a fun two days *this* had been, Mel wearily mused as she dropped into a chair at the kitchen table with a mug of tea and her laptop after finally getting her daughter to bed. The hell that was sorting through Amelia's closets, no word from Ryder and—the cherry on the sundae that was her life—Quinn's little bombshell query a half hour before.

Yeah, it was gonna take more than a cup of tea to settle her nerves after that one, she thought, wincing as she scalded her tongue. As for Ryder…she could hardly fault him for wanting time to think things through. This was a big deal, after all. Like he said, paradigm shift. And the dude never had been given to paradigm shifting just because. Of course there was also the distinct possibility he'd realized he wasn't *that* crazy. Which was fine. Really. She would, however, appreciate a head's up sometime before she turned eighty.

April's schlumping into the kitchen in a pair of baggy jammies distracted Mel from her self-torture enough to notice the adorable little frown lines marring that perfect brow. Frown lines that hadn't been in evidence earlier.

"What's up?"

Her cousin gave a short, slightly hysterical laugh. "The inspector was here this afternoon. While you were at the grocery store." Her mouth pulled down at the corners. "There's termites."

"Seriously?" Mel glanced around as though the critters were lined up on the window ledges, smacking their lips, then back at April. "Why didn't you say anything earlier?"

"Because I guess I needed time to process it all."

"All?"

"The heating system has to be replaced, too. Along with the roof."

"And thank you, Nana," Mel mumbled, then reached over to rub her cousin's shoulder. "You *sure* you want to take this on?"

That got a sigh. "At least I can afford to make the repairs. But the house's condition is really going to impact the appraisal—"

"Which it would have, anyway, even if we'd decided to sell it as a fixer-upper. Right? No sense in you paying for the repairs and *then* buying us out."

April smiled. "You're too good to me."

"And don't you forget it."

She laughed, then said, "But I really wanted to get the place up and running by Christmas, to take advantage of the Festival. Now…" She gave a tiny, defeated shrug.

"There's always my idea," Mel said.

April laughed—sort of—then shook her head. "And let the termites win? No way."

Chuckling—and declining to point out that burning the house down would not be to the termites' advantage—Mel got to her feet.

"Tea?"

"Please. And another slice of cheesecake."

Mel put the kettle on, pulled what was left of the pumpkin cheesecake out of the fridge. Yes, it was a week old by now, but any cheesecake is better than no cheesecake. *Like sex,* the termites whispered in their evil little termite voices. "This mean you have to tent the house?"

"Not sure yet. Depends on what the exterminator says. So whatcha doing?" April said with a nod toward the laptop after Mel handed her the cheesecake—which she attacked like a starving locust. Or termite—and her tea.

"Job hunting. And you might want to be careful, eat that too fast and you'll get the bends."

"I'll take my chances," April muttered around a full mouth. "Ohmigosh—I know people who'd *kill* for this."

"Not sure I'd want that on my conscience. And you'd serve cheesecake for breakfast?"

"No," she said slowly, then canted her eyes to Mel. "But I would after dinner. Since once I realized how much money I'm going to have to sink into the place I figured I might as well go for broke and turn the place back into a full-fledged inn." She lifted her fork to Mel. Staring. "With a full dinner menu."

Mel stared back. "You couldn't afford me."

"Oh, but I could. And even you have to admit Quinn's happy as a pig in slop here."

"The kid's on vacation, of course she's happy here. And that's blackmail."

"No, this is blackmail," April said, grabbing Mel's laptop, clicking a few keys, then turning the computer back to her. On which, opened in a new window, gleamed a sixty-inch, six-burner, double-oven gas stove.

In pink.

Mel gaped at her cousin, who shrugged.

"I may be little, but I'm fierce. And your pupils are dilated."

Mel blinked her pupils back to normal, then clicked away from all that gorgeousness before she weakened. "Quinn asked me tonight if her father was a sperm donor."

Now it was April's turn to gape. "Where on earth did she get that?"

"From Jack. Kid who lives a few houses down the road. Congressman's kid." At April's sorry-not-computing look, Mel said, "His mother's dead, which apparently led Quinn to share that she's missing a father. So this Jack helpfully suggested maybe I'd gone to a sperm bank, which is why I've never told her who he is."

"Holy moly. Does Quinn even know what a sperm bank is?"

"She does now," Mel said with a grimace that stretched even further when she added, "And I cannot tell you how tempting it was to just run with that hypothesis."

"But you didn't."

"No," she said, sighing heavily. "And then I changed the subject—"

"A skill at which you excel."

"—which will buy me maybe five minutes, tops. But aside from that, get this—Jack's mother and Deanna were cousins. They were killed in the same accident."

Groaning, April sagged back in her chair, tapping her fork against her now empty plate for several highly annoying seconds before saying, "So...Quinn told me about how she stayed with Ryder's father while you and Ryder went gallivanting around the countryside after the boat ride?"

"We weren't *gallivanting*. Ryder had a house call and David plied my child with ice cream."

"And you let her go?"

"I did," Mel said, trying to concentrate on the Monster.com page in front of her. With scant success, since that frickin' stove was now seared into her retinas and the make-out session with Ryder was seared into...other places.

"Oh, my word! Something happened, didn't it? Between you and Ryder? And don't you dare say 'nothing,' because your red cheeks do not lie."

Mel met her cousin's extremely amused, and equally annoying, gaze. "And this is your business, how?"

"I knew it! Oh, come on, Mel—take my mind off the termites. You wouldn't deny a poor little old widow woman the chance to live vicariously, would you?"

"Nice try. But forget it."

Her cousin's eyes narrowed. "Blythe's coming down tomorrow to show me the final drawings. And I'm not above siccing her on you."

Mel weighed that for a moment, then said, "Fine. We kissed." *Understatement.* "But it didn't mean anything." *To one of us, anyway.*

"And you're blushing again."

"Shut up—"

"So that was it? You just kissed?"

Mel waited a long time before saying. "For now," yelping when itty-bitty April smacked her forearm.

"Get out! Y'all are gonna do the deed?"

"Maybe. And you are way too excited about this."

"And you're not? Mel!" April wagged her hands. "This is Ryder you're talking about—!"

"Who's still hung up on his fiancée. Remember?"

"Ohhh. Right." She sighed. "Guess that puts a different spin on things."

"You might say."

"So you'd be fine with a fling?" This said with the kind of dubious expression one might employ for, say, someone who'd just suggested sledding down Everest. On a flattened cardboard box.

"You kidding? I'd be *thrilled* with a fling."

"With anybody? Or with Ryder?"

"Yeesh, give me *some* credit."

"Just checking."

"Look, I totally get that Ry's head and body aren't in

the same place. I know that, I'm good with that, even, but I'm not sure he is. You loved your husband—you understand, right, how hard this must be for him?"

Something flickered in April's eyes before she wrapped her hand around Mel's. "I understand how hard this is for *you*."

"Me? I told you—"

"Frankly, if I was in your shoes, I don't know that I wouldn't do the same thing. But I also think you're fooling yourself, if you think you can make love with Ryder and then walk away like it was nothing. That's just not you, honey."

Back to Monster. "And maybe I've changed."

After a moment April got up to carry her plate to the sink and wash it. "Lying to me is one thing. But to yourself? That's something else entirely."

The doorbell dinged but forgot to dong. Lordamercy, was there anything in this house that didn't have to be replaced?

Sighing, Mel tromped to the door. Opened it. Fell head first down the rabbit hole that was Ryder's dark, conflicted gaze.

"I thought things through," he said.

Chapter Eight

"You're sure April's okay with sitting?" Ryder asked over his break-dancing pulse as they parked the car by the nearly deserted marina.

"Of course," Mel answered—as she'd done all three times he'd asked—even though Ryder hadn't missed her cousin's concerned gaze as they walked out the door. Yes, even though he'd also caught Mel's mouthed, "I'll be fine," a moment before. "Quinn's been dead asleep for an hour, at least. Kid's down for the count until seven."

Ryder got out of the car and was around to Mel's side before she could open her own door, grabbing her hand and hauling her to her feet, the brisk breeze blowing her bangs off her face. Moonlight speared the pewter clouds, glancing off the motley assortment of small boats languidly bobbing in the night-black water as she smiled up at him.

"You're shaking," she said, her hand soft, warm against his face. "Look, we don't have to—"

"I know. Except...I do."

She took his hand and tugged him toward the boat, their footsteps too loud against the dock. Her suggestion, not his, as though she'd understood how hard it would have been for him to take her to the house.

He helped her on board, shivering from both the chill and the anticipation. But when she tried to hug him, he shook his head.

"Not yet."

She sat beside him as he drove the cuddy out into the bay, to the group of islands they'd passed two days before, to moor at a private dock behind a house he knew had been vacant for months. Silence enveloped them, save for the gentle lapping of water against the boat's hull, the occasional hoot of an owl.

"It's gorgeous," Mel whispered. "Perfect."

Ryder cleared his throat. "I brought wine—"

"Don't need wine. Thanks."

"—and condoms."

She chuckled. "Those, we can use."

His heart jackhammering, Ryder led her into the tiny cabin, the ceiling too low for him to stand upright. He switched on a low light, a small heater, then tossed a cotton blanket across the puzzle of cushions that made up the sleeping area. Then he sat, as if not sure what came next.

Mel kneeled on the bed beside him, taking his face in her hands. "Hey," she whispered. "No pressure. I'm fine with making out. Or sitting outside and admiring the scenery, whatever works for you—"

He silenced her with a kiss, easing her onto the bed, and she opened her mouth, inviting, making sweet little noises in her throat that made him crazy, made his eyes burn—

"It's okay, touching's allowed," she whispered, and he

slipped his hand underneath her hoodie, and she jerked, laughing. "Cold!"

"Sorry—"

"No, keep going, things'll warm up soon enough...*oh.* Yes. Like that."

He responded almost immediately.

Smiling, Mel pressed one hand to his chest. "So we're good?"

When he nodded, she pushed herself up to toe off her Crocs, unzip her jeans, the rocking boat throwing her off balance as she wriggled free. On a startled laugh she grabbed the bulkhead and kicked the jeans behind her, then straddled him, pure devilment in her eyes, her grin, as she slowly unzipped her hoodie. At his undoubtedly stunned expression, she laughed.

"Worth the wait?"

"I'm a doctor, it's not as if I haven't seen..." Ryder swallowed, then laughed. "I'm speechless."

"Good thing, then, this isn't a debate," Mel said, leaning closer—oh, man—to thread her fingers through his hair before joining their mouths, her kiss soft and teasing and making him feel like a rutting teenager. Especially when her nipples got cozy with his chest and every ounce of blood in his body roared south to its happy place, taking any vestige of control right along with it.

Annoyed with himself, Ryder clamped her shoulders in some lame attempt to separate them, except Mel planted her hands on either side of his head and locked their gazes. "Hey. This is my gift to you. Whatever you want, however you want it, I'm just along for the ride. And trust me, *fast* is not a problem—"

He was naked and sheathed and inside her within seconds.

So much for not wanting to rush things.

And yet, amazingly, she cried out before he did, her fingers digging into his bare shoulders as she spasmed underneath, around, *through* him, and he buried his face in her neck, so close, aching to be closer, vaguely aware of her breath coming in short little pants, hot in his ear, and she laced her ankles at the small of his back to pull him in harder and deeper until there was only pleasure, only *this,* bright and hot and blinding.

Tears stung as he drove into her, recklessly, relentlessly, startled when she came a second time, the pulsing finally driving him over an edge he'd shied away from for more than a year.

Afterwards they lay in the dim light, a tangle of sweaty limbs and racing hearts, the boat gently pitching beneath them, until Mel broke the silence with, "Feel better?"

Ryder expelled a short laugh. "I'll let you know in a minute." He looked over to see Mel's eyes trained on his face, her expression unreadable, and shame slammed through the afterglow. His gut cramping, Ryder traced a knuckle down her cheek. "That wasn't exactly finessed."

"After a year? I should hardly think so."

"You deserve better than that."

"Oh, for the love of Mike…" Mel flopped onto her side, palming his chest. "Okay. I've got this cookie recipe that has like, I don't know, twenty steps and twelve ingredients, takes all freaking afternoon to make. Granted, the end result is to die for. But sometimes I'm all about ripping open a bag of Betty Crocker mix, adding an egg and some butter, and boom—ten minutes later, cookies. And you know what? When you want *those* cookies, *those* cookies are every bit as satisfying as the ones that take forever."

Ryder mirrored her position to rest his hand on her hip. Her firm round hip which he'd been too preoccupied before to thoroughly appreciate. Along with the rest of this *gift,* as she called it.

Carefully, deliberately, he slid his hand down her thigh, then back up over her hip again, to her waist, then her breast, warm and soft and irresistible, watching her brows lift, her mouth curve.

"So do you ever get a yen for both kinds of cookies at the same time?" he asked, and she laughed, that wonderful, throaty sound that wrapped around his wounded heart like thick, warm fleece on a stormy night.

"Oh, yeah."

"Glad to hear it," he said, shifting to kiss her.

In a spot, that, judging from her squeal, she clearly hadn't expected.

If Ryder fast was amazing, Ryder slow was...

Was...

Can I get back to you on that? Mel mused drowsily a looooong time later, cradled against that lovely, solid chest, his lovely, strong heart thumping steadily in her ear, even as she knew at any moment the endorphins would wear off and she'd realize she was in a whole heap o' trouble. Not to mention while they'd been satiating the heck out of each other all that other stuff hadn't magically resolved itself.

But until then...

Bliss.

"I suppose I should get you back to the house," he murmured, tracing lovely, lacey circles on her shoulder. "Or April will wonder."

Mel chuckled. "Wonder, nothing. April *knows.*"

Although Ryder's flinch might've been nearly imperceptible if she hadn't been smooshed up beside him, all nekkid and what-all, a flinch, it definitely was. "Knows?"

"That we didn't pop out to IHOP for a late-night snack."

He sighed. "Which would no doubt account for the scathing look she gave me."

"Can April even do scathing?"

"Apparently so."

"She's afraid I'll get my heart broken. Even though I assured her that wouldn't happen." At Ryder's silence, she thought, *Oh, hell,* and shifted to look at him. Mustered up the courage to ask, "Were you thinking about her? When we—"

Dude looked thoroughly confused. "Who? April?"

"No."

His sudden grip on her arm was almost painful. "Let's get one thing straight, Mel—I have never in my life had sex with one woman while fantasizing about another. Whatever went on tonight was between us. Period."

Then she saw it. The misgiving, radiating like a damn aura.

"However...?"

He curled forward, plunging a hand through his hair, and Mel would have given almost anything to be stricken deaf at that moment. So she wouldn't have had to hear him say, "This was still probably a mistake."

"A mistake, it should be noted, it took you more than an *hour* to figure out."

He twisted to look at her, his expression ravaged. "I don't do hook-ups, either."

"Is that what you think this was? A *hook-up?*"

"Wasn't it?"

Annoyed as all hell—with him, with herself, with the whole damn situation—Mel lunged forward to search for her clothes scattered across what there was of the floor in the minuscule cabin, knocking the wind out of herself in the process. Panties and jeans found, she clumsily jerked them back on, then grabbed the hoodie.

"Okay, bub, let *me* make something clear—" she shoved her arms into the hoodie, jerked up the zipper "—while I'm more than aware that this was a one-shot deal, believe me, I don't give just anybody access to these—" she pointed to her boobs "—let alone the rest of the package. But if you don't think what we just shared was a rare and wonderful thing...well, I don't suppose I can tell you what to think, can I?"

His own clothes yanked back on, Ryder followed Mel up onto the deck. "And you being upset right now only proves how wrong it was."

Mel wheeled on him, only to lift her hands and suck in a deep breath. Then another. Before she clobbered him like she used to when they were kids. "I'm not upset because of what we did, birdbrain, I'm upset because you're being an *idiot*."

"And maybe that's my point!" Ryder shot back, then shoved out a lungful of air. "I'm sorry—"

"For what?"

He gave her an exasperated look. "I thought doing that...with you...would, I don't know. Purge me. Or something. Force me out of this prison I can't seem to leave even though I know I'm the one holding the key. Instead, now I know I can't *make* the doors open. And it kills me that...that I used you."

"Even though I was more than willing to be used?"

"Not sure how that makes it better. Let alone right."

"Oh, Ry, Ry, Ry..." Mel huffed out a breath, then grabbed the railing to keep her balance as the boat lurched. "You are too damn good for your *own* good, you know that? When are you going to stop shouldering the responsibility for everybody else's decisions?"

"I don't—"

"Yes, you do. You always have. I used to find it admirable. Now I just want to slap you silly."

He almost smiled. "It's just…" After a short head shake, he glanced down, then back at her. "I thought, here we are starting over, trying to figure out what we are to each other, to…to forge something solid for Quinn's sake if nothing else, and now…" His shoulders jerked with the force of his sigh. "I was afraid we'd ruined our chance at a do-over. That *I'd* ruined it."

"For crying out loud—are you *listening* to yourself? Like you said, what we are to each other and what you are, or will be, to Quinn…separate issues. So. Did you have a good time tonight?"

Ryder looked out over the water, his jaw clenching, before letting his gaze touch hers again. "Goes without saying."

"Then could you simply own that and not overthink it, for heaven's sake?"

Another several seconds passed before, at long last, his scowl relaxed. Not exactly into a smile, but at least he no longer looked as though he'd accidentally set World War Three in motion.

"I'll try," he said, and Mel released another breath.

"It's a step," she said, even as she sternly told her heart to listen up, to own her own decision, her own actions, for what they were—nothing more than simply helping out a friend in need.

That she'd known going in that *more* was not an option, so no moaning about it now.

Granted, their attempts at normal conversation on the short drive back to Amelia's house were pretty abysmal, but considering all the stuff churning in Mel's head, she could only imagine what was going through Ryder's. She could reassure him until the cows came home, but ultimately he was responsible for finding his own peace.

"You don't have to get out," she said when they pulled up in front of the house, but he did anyway. 'Cause that's the kind of guy he was.

Even took her hand when he walked her to the door, yeesh. Which did not make things *less* strained between them. Once there, however, he let go to ram his hands in his pockets, his distressed gaze steady in hers. "I can't even begin to tell you how much you mean to me," he said quietly, and her heart ka-thudded against her sternum. "How much…" He removed one hand from his pocket to drag it across his downturned mouth before slugging it back into its cave. "How much I…appreciated tonight." Could be a trick of the light, but she could have sworn his eyes glimmered. "How grateful I am it was you."

Her own smile was a little wobbly. "Kinda the point I was trying to make?"

Ryder blew a laugh through his nose. "You're something else, Mel Duncan," he said, then walked back to his car, his footsteps the loneliest sound Mel had ever heard.

And perfectly echoing her own heartbeat.

Except for the occasional fitful, fretful patch of sleep, Ryder had lain awake most of the night, becoming more irritated with each chime of the grandfather clock—another flea market find—downstairs.

Because for all the words he and Mel had tossed at each other after their little tryst, the truth—at least on his part—had deftly sidestepped them all, flitting in and out of the conversation like a ghost. Now, at some unholy hour of the morning as he poured himself a cup of brutally black coffee in the cold, half-finished kitchen, the apparition shimmered more clearly into focus. Still elusive, for sure, but whose unsettling existence he couldn't deny.

Ryder shut his eyes, not against the specter, but so he could will it more clearly into focus, despite the raging headache, and heartache, it brought with it:

That even though he knew he couldn't be what Mel needed and deserved, he wanted her. Especially after last night. Selfishly, irrationally, like a child obsessed with the idea of having something he can't take proper care of.

Because the thing was, he knew Mel too well, knew she was lying about being okay with last night's one-off. As generous as she was, she wasn't *that* generous—as her own admission about how seldom she shared her body attested, he thought with a tight grin. And *he'd* be lying if he didn't admit how much that admission had stoked his ego, even as it made mincemeat out of his already pummeled heart.

Ryder took another swig of the bitter brew, an equally bitter laugh escaping his throat as he thought of what Mel's reaction would be to his musings. At this point, "slapping him silly" seemed fitting, somehow, especially when it hit him that he'd somehow landed right where he'd been ten years ago. Why was it, he wondered, did *he* keep being what he most had to protect her from?

Irony, he thought that was called.

Although this time he couldn't turn tail and run. Nor did he want to. For good or ill he was crazy about this sleepy little town, loved how his practice here was more about people than paperwork and peddling quick "fixes" that rarely were, about being able to offer comfort when there was little else to offer. So Mel's determination not to stick around any longer than necessary was actually a godsend…and at least part of the impetus behind Ryder's resolve, that gray, gloomy morning, to settle this issue about Quinn without further delay.

The other being, of course, his promise to Mel to do what he could to fix this whole sorry mess. Even if that meant alienating his mother—not that he had a whole lot to lose there, he thought peevishly. But if what his father had intimated to Mel was true, if Lorraine was still hanging on to secrets that had in all likelihood played, or were still playing, some part in said mess, then Ryder would do everything in his power to drag them out of her, once and for all and damn the torpedoes. At least he could give Mel that.

He waited until seven, however, to call the woman who'd given him life, both to be sure she was awake and after having consumed enough caffeine to fuel the entire Eastern Shore. She answered on the fourth ring, breathing hard.

"Ry? Why on earth are you calling so early? Is everything okay?"

"I'm fine. Are you?"

"What? Oh, of course. I took the dogs for a walk, the phone was ringing when we got in, I ran to get it—"

"So you haven't had breakfast yet?"

"No. Why?"

"Thought I'd join you."

"Oh. Um, sure. Your father's gone though, he had a delivery last night—"

"That's fine, it's you I want to talk to."

"Really?" A pause. "Actually, since I wanted to talk to you, too, this is good. Don't hurry, though, I look a fright."

A half hour later, Ryder was seated at the round, whitewashed table in the breakfast room in front of a plate of Eggbeaters and toast with some supposedly heart-healthy spread. His parents never replaced Maureen and Tony, opting instead for weekly visits from yard and housekeeping services, his mother declaring it was time she learned how to cook, anyway—after a fashion—although holidays and dinner parties were always catered.

Pulled together in a pair of gray pants and a lavender sweater that clashed violently with her red hair, Lorraine sat across from him, buttering her toast and looking eerily cheerful. "This is nice, don't you think? We so rarely have breakfast together anymore." They'd rarely had breakfast together, ever, but Ryder let it go. "So why are you here?"

"To discuss Quinn," he said, and his mother's eyes shot to his. "It's time to put this whole nonsense to bed, don't you think?"

His mother took a sip of her coffee, the creamy, gold-rimmed Lenox cup rattling slightly when she set it back on the saucer. "Well. Nothing like coming straight to the point."

"I thought so."

His mother's eyes lifted to his, sharp with her customary determination. And something else, something that both caught him slightly off guard and put him on it. But before he could figure out what, she said, "I saw her yesterday."

His glass of fresh-squeezed orange juice halfway to his mouth, Ryder jerked. "Excuse me?"

"At Finnegan's. Your father texted me, told me they were there. Don't be angry," she said when Ryder's brows crashed, "I think he thought I might not get another chance to see her." In the stark morning light, her blush was unmistakable. "And I wrestled with myself for several minutes before curiosity won out over..." She paused. "Over habit. So I went. But I sat at a table a few feet away so she wouldn't see me. Or at least, so she wouldn't have any reason to guess who I was if she did."

Lorraine nibbled her toast, rubbing non-existent crumbs from her fingers when she set the piece back on her plate, then let her gaze drift out the window. "She's quite something, isn't she?"

Bowled over both by this bit of information and the wistfulness in her voice, Ryder sat back in his chair. It couldn't possibly be this easy, could it?

"Yes. She is."

She looked back at him, then lifted one hand to her hair, her diamonds glittering. "You're absolutely right, it is time to put this all behind us. I know how badly I've bungled things—"

"To say the least."

Her nostrils flared with her sigh. "When we found out Jeremy had gotten Melanie pregnant," she said, "it all seemed so wrong. On so many levels. I really did what I thought was best, you have to believe that. But had I realized…"

She glanced down at the oblivious retriever lying beside her, then back up at Ryder. "I want to know my granddaughter. I want to be her grandmother. Especially since Jeremy and Caroline have decided not to have children, and you…" She bit down on whatever she'd been about to say.

"In other words, you think Quinn's your only shot."

"I didn't say that."

"You didn't have to."

"I'm a realist, Ryder. I deal with what's in front of me, not what might be. And who knows how long it's going to take you to get over Deanna—"

"Not here to talk about Deanna, Mom," Ryder said, refusing to let her derail the conversation. Or let his own issues taint it. "Or me. And I suppose you're right—you can only work with what you're given. In fact, one of the reasons *I* want to see this resolved is because I'm already nuts about Quinn, too. But I want a real relationship with her, not one based on lies and secrets. I want her to know

I'm her uncle. However, that's not going to happen until you make things up to Mel. Yes, that's right—you want access to your granddaughter, you're going to have deal with Mel." Images flashed, receded. As did a flash-fire of longing Ryder literally swallowed down. "And me."

His mother gave him a speculative look. "So your friendship…it's back on?"

"It would seem so," he said carefully, even as guilt wrapped icy cold fingers around his heart and squeezed tight. "And whatever my role in all this is, it's as her advocate."

A smile crept across his mother's mouth. "Meaning you're my only hope for fixing this."

"Only to a certain extent. The rest is up to you."

"But she's at least amenable to the idea? That we're all on the same page—?"

"Not so fast. Yes, she's definitely ready to tell Quinn the truth, especially since she keeps asking about her father—"

"Oh, no—we can't bring Jeremy into this."

"Not sure how you think you're going to keep him out. Since not only is it Quinn's right to know whose genes she's carrying, if she finds out you're her grandparents, and I'm not her father, that kind of leaves a pretty big X factor in the equation, don't you think?"

His mother grimaced. "But his marriage…"

"Not our problem, Mom. Not *your* problem. Because guess what? Jeremy's all grown up now." At least, ostensibly. "He will deal, because he has no choice. And so will Caroline."

His mother knuckled the rapidly deepening wrinkle between her brows, then let her hand smack to the table. "God. Secrets are a bitch."

"And there's a revelation that's eleven years too late."

Her eyes shot to his. And there it was again, that look,

like some creature furtively peeking out of a door that had been locked for far too long. "Fine. Just let me...warn him."

"No, actually, I call that one."

"Ryder, no, this has nothing to do with you—"

"Oh, yeah? Jeremy damn well knew how important Mel was to me. So you can't tell me his moving in on her like a cheetah with a wounded gazelle wasn't deliberate. As angry as I am with you, that's got nothing on how I feel about him."

His mother fidgeted with her juice glass. "Then why didn't you call him as soon as you found out?"

"Because Mel would've killed me," he said, and his mother almost smiled. "But before you go planning Quinn's coming-out party, there's a huge gap between telling Quinn who you are and letting her get chummy with you."

His mother looked more chagrined than hurt. "But I... we could give the child so much—"

"To make up for what you stole from her, you mean."

His mother's cheeks colored. "I suppose I deserved that."

"Yes. You do."

"But Mel doesn't seem to have a problem letting Quinn be around your father."

"Actually, she did. But at least I think she trusts Dad. You? Not so much. And why should she?" He leaned forward. "Did you think Mel wouldn't tell me how you treated her? The despicable things you said to her? You did more than hurt Mel, Mother. You made her feel worthless. It's going to take more than a simple apology to undo this damage. In fact, the word *groveling* comes to mind. Especially when you factor in what this little fiasco cost her mother. What you did—"

"For God's sake, Ryder! I get it!" Shaking, Lorraine

pushed herself up from the table and crossed the slate floor to one of the windows overlooking the leaf-flecked backyard and the water beyond, her arms tightly crossed over her ribs. The dogs heaved themselves to their feet and followed, worried. "I panicked, Ryder. And I know that's no excuse, but..."

"But what?" When she pressed her lips together a second time, Ryder rose as well to come up beside her. "You may as well know...Dad already intimated to Mel that there's more going on here than the obvious." His mother's startled eyes shot to his. "And no, I have no clue what that might be. But whatever the truth is, you owe it to her. Because without it, you can probably kiss any shot of having a real relationship with Quinn goodbye."

"Boy's right, Lorraine," his father said from the doorway, making both of them spin around. Rumpled and obviously drained, David crossed to the buffet and poured himself a cup of coffee. "Half-assed isn't going to cut it." He lifted the cup to her. "Time to air the dirty laundry."

Blushing furiously, Lorraine glanced at Ryder, then back at her husband. "But you said—"

"What I said more than thirty years ago," his father said in the most forceful voice Ryder had ever heard, "has no bearing whatsoever on the present." Then his expression softened. "Besides...there's nothing to hold you back anymore, is there?"

Several seconds passed. Then, her eyes trained on David, as though trying to absorb strength from him, Lorraine finally said, "It doesn't have anything to do with Mel directly." Her gaze swung to Ryder. "But it does involve her grandmother. And..." She sucked in a breath. "And what I did to her."

Chapter Nine

"You do realize it's freezing out here?"

Hunkered down in one of the weather-ravaged Adirondack chairs on the equally weather-ravaged back porch, Mel aimed a wan smile from inside her fleece hood at Blythe, standing in the doorway leading from the gathering room. And who, in her ridiculously high-heeled ankle boots—how did anybody walk in those things?—and artfully draped layers looked like a damn goddess. As opposed to Mel, who felt more like a troll. With a hangover. And cramps.

"Suits my mood," Mel said, looking back over the gloomy landscape, the sky and water the same shade of leaden gray, one eagle eye trained on Quinn and her new friend. "You just get in?"

"A few minutes ago, yeah." Blythe rearranged several of the layers to sit in another chair a few feet away, a magnum of designer coffee clutched to her chest. "Can only stay a little while, though. Got an appointment in Falls Church this afternoon." Mel grunted. "Who's the kid with Quinn?"

"Name's Jack something. Father's a newish congressman in Washington."

"Wes Phillips?"

"That would be him. He seems okay." She'd actually met the boy earlier, fed him cookies, tried to get him to talk, decided the sperm bank mention was probably as bad as it was going to get. Then Mel felt a smile push at her unwilling lips. "The kid, I mean, haven't met the dad. He's off legislating. Or whatever our tax dollars pay them to do. I think they're plotting world domination," she said, watching her daughter and the boy, deep in conversation out on the pier. "The kids, I mean. Not congress. Then again…"

Blythe chuckled, then sobered. "So April tells me you went out with Ryder last night?"

Just who she wanted to talk about. The text a half hour ago had been short and to the point, that his mother wanted to "chat." Mel cut her eyes to her cousin, then sank further into her grumpfest. "April sic you on me?"

"Wouldn't be out here freezing my butt off otherwise. And I'm guessing 'went out with' is a euphemism?"

"We went out. On a boat, even."

Blythe snorted. Elegantly, of course. "And you don't think this is going to complicate things? With Quinn?"

"Not that this is any of your business, but it was a one-shot deal. An agreed-upon one-shot-deal, at that. So, no. No complications here."

"For Quinn? Or you?"

"Anybody," Mel said, staring really hard at all that gray.

Because damn her cute little hide, April had been right. If Mel had never been a fan of just-for-fun sex before, what on earth made her think she'd be okay with it now? Even with Ryder? *Especially* with Ryder—? "You tell her yet?"

"Working up to it. I've got a job interview in Baltimore next week, so before then. Depends on…things."

"As in, the Caldwells?"

Mel turned to her cousin. "I assume April's already told you that Quinn met Ryder's father. With whom she instantly bonded, natch. And the thing is…" She looked away again. "He'd make a terrific grandfather. I always did like Dr. David. There's a good guy there."

"Despite his collusion?" Mel felt Blythe's eyes on the side of her face. Or her hoodie, in this case. For a long time. Until Mel finally tugged back the edge of the hood to peer at her cousin. "What?"

"I know you always wondered about Nana's issues with Aunt Maureen."

Mel frowned. "Not really. It was pretty obvious she was irked because Mom went to work for the Caldwells—"

"Apparently it went way beyond that," Blythe said quietly as a besweatered April joined them on the porch, struggling to shut the stubborn patio door behind her before coming to stand beside Mel. Who looked from one to the other, her stomach doing a slow, nauseating turn.

"What's going on?"

"Not what's going on," April said, squatting beside Mel's knees. "What *went* on. Long before any of us were born. You remember those boxes of papers Blythe and I divided up?"

"Yeah…"

Blythe dug inside underneath her many layers of garments to pull out a brittle, yellowing piece of paper which she handed to Mel. "I found this among them."

Lorraine was stacking the few breakfast dishes into the dishwasher when the doorbell rang, making her jump out of her skin and the dogs to their feet, barking.

"Lucy! Ethel! Quiet!"

Already unnerved from the little family meeting that morning, she hurried to the front of the house, the dogs hot on her heels as the chime bong-bonged over and over, as though someone was in dire straits on the other side. David and Ryder had already left for work; the cleaning service wasn't due for another hour yet. Sunlight streamed through the clerestory windows in the two-story foyer as Lorraine opened the door…and felt every drop of blood drain from her face.

"Melanie!"

Cheeks ablaze, eyes sparking, the young woman thrust a folded-up piece of paper practically in Lorraine's face.

"You had an affair with my *grandfather?*"

Oh, hell. Not this way. Not—

"Why don't you come in…?"

"All those names you called me, all that crap you accused me of, when *you'd* slept with *someone else's husband!* So not only were you a snob, but a hypocrite, to boot—!"

"And we are not having this conversation on my doorstep," Lorraine said, attempting to regain control of the situation. She stepped aside, gesturing toward the foyer. "In. Now." The dogs wisely stumbled out of Mel's way as she torpedoed inside. "Go straight ahead—"

"To the den, got it."

Lorraine followed Mel into the same room where they'd had a certain discussion all those years ago, gesturing to the sofa. "Have a seat."

"Not necessary," Mel said as she scanned the room before spearing Lorraine with her gaze, definitely not the same cowering young woman who'd stood here then. "Nothing's changed, I see."

"More than you might guess, actually," Lorraine said, willing her racing heart to still. "I was going to tell you—"

"Yeah, right—"

"I was. You beat me to it." She looked down at the letter, still in Mel's hands. "Where did you find that?"

"I didn't, my cousin did. In my grandmother's things." At the pain and anger—every bit entirely justifiable—in the young woman's eyes, Lorraine felt her own sting.

"May I see it?"

"Go right ahead," Mel said, handing her the letter. "Although I imagine you probably know it by heart. Since you wrote it."

"Very true. On both counts," Lorraine said, carefully unfolding the brittle paper. Her best vellum, a wedding gift from some aunt or other, long dead. Her handwriting had been prettier then. Neater. Her heart cramping, she scanned the apology Amelia Rinehart had demanded she write, three years almost to the day before Ryder's birth, her promise to never see or speak to George Rinehart again. A promise she'd had no trouble keeping, as it happened—Lorraine had been stupid and George a womanizing bastard who apparently continued to assault Lorraine's dignity with pathetic regularity for the rest of his life. But while Amelia had never been able to control her philandering husband, she'd held a hatchet over Lorraine's head for the rest of *her* life.

She refolded the letter, tried to hand it back. Her arms crossed, Mel shook her head. "That's all right, you keep it."

Lorraine set it on a nearby lamp table, tapping her fingers on the polished wood surface for a moment before lifting her eyes to Mel's. "For what it's worth, it didn't last long. And I ended it."

"But who started it?"

"It was…mutual."

"My God, he must've been, what? Thirty years older than you?"

She laughed without humor. "I suppose that was part of the allure." When Mel pulled a face, she said, "I was a newlywed, very young and very lonely—David was away a lot, doing his residency at Johns Hopkins. For two years I rarely saw him, and when I did, he was distracted. And exhausted—"

"Which was no excuse to cheat on him."

"Of course it wasn't. But I was a spoiled daddy's girl who had no clue how to deal with real life," Lorraine said sharply. "Or how to resist temptation. So I made a dreadful error in judgment. One your grandmother never let me forget."

"Does Ryder's father know?"

She nodded. "I told him. Some time before your grandmother found out, in fact."

That seemed to take Mel aback. "And he—"

"Forgave me? Eventually. And a helluva lot more easily than I forgave myself."

For all Mel really, really wanted to hate Lorraine, with every passing minute the fury slipped away a little more. Not that she was ready to fall on Ry's mother's freckled neck and forgive her—woman still had a whole lot of 'splainin' to do—but damned if she wasn't beginning to see her as almost human. Who knew?

"You really never saw my grandfather again?"

"I saw him, of course. It's a small town. But spoke to him? Not one word."

Finally Mel sat on the edge of the sofa, distractedly playing with one dog's ears when the beast wedged herself between the sofa and the coffee table to lay her head on Mel's knees, her big brown eyes nearly as importunate as her mistress's. And slowly but surely things began to make sense. "But that wasn't enough for my grandmother."

"No. As far as she was concerned, what had been done couldn't be undone."

"Yeah," she conceded, "that was Nana, all right. Which was why…crap." Her face lifted to Lorraine's. "Why she could never forgive my mother for marrying my father and coming to work for you."

Lorraine walked over to a small chest by the window, littered with silver-framed family photos, her nervous toying with them reminding Mel so much of Quinn she nearly lost her breath. "Honestly, I had no idea Tony and Maureen were even seeing each other—I guess Maureen somehow knew Amelia wouldn't approve. First I found out about it was after their marriage—you know they eloped?"

"Lord, yes. Mom only told me the story a hundred times."

A slight smile touched Lorraine's lips. "My housekeeper had just retired. Maureen volunteered to replace her. And afterwards, there were…scenes."

"With my grandmother?"

"Yes. She accused me of 'stealing' your mother the same way I'd stolen your grandfather. Even though years had passed since then. And when you were born and Ryder glommed on to you…" Abruptly, Lorraine walked over to the armchair across from Mel and sank onto it, her hands tightly folded in her lap. "Your mother and I both knew Amelia would blow a gasket, but we figured the novelty would pass, that he'd soon lose interest in you. When he didn't…"

Her mouth pressed tight, Lorraine looked at her lap.

"What?"

Her eyes lifted. "Before you were born, Ryder was very quiet. Too quiet. In fact, he barely spoke. David and I took him to every specialist and child psychologist imaginable, and they all said the same thing, that there was nothing physically or neurologically wrong, that he'd outgrow it eventually. Then you came, and he blossomed. No one had any rational explanation for that, either."

Stunned, Mel froze, not moving again until the dog nudged her hand for another pat. "So that's why you turned a blind eye to our friendship."

Lorraine hmmphed. "Blind? Hardly. But within a few months of your birth he was like any other child his age. So his father and I were actually very grateful to you. And no, Ryder doesn't know, since we never said anything."

"So you're saying my grandmother never knew about Ryder and me?"

"No. Your mother and I…we made sure of it. That he never went over to Amelia's to see you girls unless she wasn't there. Or that your mother would pick you all up first when you went on your little…" She smiled. "Excursions."

"Then why the hell did you—"

"Treat you like dirt?" Lorraine's eyes glistened. "Do you have any idea how impressed I am, that you're here?"

"Excuse me?"

"If I'd had half your balls back then none of this would've happened. But I didn't. And I know you have no reason to trust me, or believe me, even, especially considering all those awful things I said to you. But when your grandmother found out what happened, she blamed me. And she threatened to tell everyone in our circle 'the truth' if I didn't send you—and your mother—away."

"Wait…" Mel frowned. "Are you saying she knew I was pregnant before you did?"

Lorraine lifted a hand to her throat, a tear slipping down her cheek. "Yes."

"How—?"

"Because your mother told her."

Her breath leaving her lungs in a rush, Mel collapsed against the back of the sofa. Holy hell. "Why on earth would she do that?"

Lorraine plucked a dog hair off her knee. "Were you aware your mother was trying to reconcile with Amelia?"

"What? No."

The older woman nodded, then sighed. "Your father's death shook your mother to the core. Which you know. And I think it hit her that she didn't have forever to repair the relationship with her mother. And that it was up to her to make it happen, if it was going to happen at all. She had no idea, of course, about...about what had happened between your grandfather and me. And I seriously doubt that Amelia told her."

"So you're saying the reconciliation took?"

"They'd begun to talk, I know that much."

"Enough that my mother felt she could confide in Nana that I was pregnant?" When Lorraine shrugged, Mel belted out a harsh laugh. "Ryder's and my friendship, she kept in the closet, yet she told her I was carrying Jeremy's kid. That's rich."

"I didn't say it made sense. And your mother...she was still grieving. I don't think she was thinking straight in those days. She probably thought there was no one else she could tell."

Mel sat up, pressing her fingertips into her temples. "And Nana used it against you."

"Basically, yes. You see, in her mind her husband's cheating reflected negatively on her almost as much as it did on him. And of course I wasn't exactly keen on anyone discovering my indiscretion. So for a long time we both had a stake in making sure the truth stayed well hidden."

"Hence her making you promise to keep quiet about it."

"Exactly. But at George's death, she discovered…" She blushed again.

"That you hadn't been the only one."

Lorraine nodded. "At which point outing me would have been no skin off her nose. But it still would have been off mine. Not that I didn't want to protect Jeremy— heaven knows I'm not laying the entire blame for this at your grandmother's feet. And I was ashamed, and morti- fied. But—"

"Nana held it over your head," Mel breathed out.

Hope shone in the older woman's eyes. "So you do be- lieve me?"

"Considering that Nana never spoke to me again? Never responded when I sent her pictures of Quinn after she was born?" She felt her mouth pull to one side. "That if I'm being honest, I remember my grandfather flirting with every female over sixteen who crossed his path? Yeah. I believe you. *But…*"

Mel stood, stepping over the dog to cross to the same window, picking up a picture of darling Jeremy and his cute, perfect, Asian wife, the silver frame cold in her hand. "All this time, I've beaten myself up for *my* mistake, for the misery I caused my mother before she'd even had five minutes to come to terms with my father's death. Not that she ever admitted that to my face, but I knew. Not only that I'd disappointed her, but that my actions had forced her out of what she thought of as her own home. And she did love this place. This house," she said, glancing around before replacing the photo, then once more leveling her gaze on Lorraine. "Leaving it…it devastated her. So it might've been nice to know that it wasn't entirely my fault."

"You don't understand—as long as your grandmother was alive, I didn't dare tell anyone the truth—"

"That's bull, Lorraine. You still had choices—"

"What choices? Your grandmother...you were still a kid, you probably didn't realize how much influence she could still wield in this town. She could have ruined things for us—"

"Not to the point that you couldn't have gotten in touch with me, or my mother, at any time and explained. Apologized. If it's true Nana never told my mother what her real beef with you was, then Mom had no idea, either, why you reacted the way you did. Or, hell, why Nana never spoke to her again. If they had begun to mend fences—ohmigod, that must've devastated my mother. So at least we would have understood. *I* would have understood."

"I was ashamed, Mel," Lorraine said softly. "I still am."

"Sorry. Not good enough."

After a moment Lorraine stood and walked over to Mel, her arms folded over her ribs. "David saw to Amelia's medical needs in her last years. By then she'd alienated everyone she'd ever known. And, according to him, she died a lonely, bitter old woman with, as he put it, only her grudges to keep her company."

"That, and every item anyone's ever hawked on QVC," Mel muttered, and Lorraine sadly smiled.

"I don't want to end up like that, Mel. Having no one give a damn about me." Then she sighed. "I'd also like to think Amelia can't hurt us anymore. But now I'm not so sure."

Mel's face warmed, even as she acknowledged the thing writhing inside her, grown fat and sassy with all the nurturing and coddling and encouragement she'd given it over the years. The only thing she'd been able to count on, she realized with a start. Well, hell.

"What I don't get," she said, almost more to herself than

Lorraine, "is why Nana left me the house. If she disapproved of me so much—"

"Because it was never about you, Melanie. It was about me. And maybe, in your grandmother's head, this was her way of making it up to you? Sounds crazy, I know, but after all she let you stay with your cousins all those summers, despite her rift with your mother. My guess is she did love you, in her own way."

"As in, *bizarre* and *demented?*" Mel muttered, and Lorraine softly laughed.

"You know what I think? That your grandfather hurt her deeply. As I did David," she said, her eyes brimming again. "But at least I've done everything in my power to atone for my reprehensible behavior." Color flooded her cheeks. "To him, at least. Now all I ask is that you let me do the same thing for you. And Quinn?" She unfolded her arms, briefly reaching for Mel before seeming to rethink the gesture. "Come to dinner, both of you. Tomorrow night. Say, seven? What's Quinn's favorite food?"

"Anything but raisins, but—"

"Then it's settled," Lorraine said, finally touching Mel's arm to steer her out of the room, toward the front door.

Settled? Not by a long shot. Even if Mel had gotten some long overdue answers. Still...

"The wounds...they go pretty deep, Lorraine. So you'll understand if I still don't entirely trust you."

"Completely," she said, disappointment wrestling with hope in her eyes. "But...?"

"But...yes, we'll come to dinner. And we'll take it from there, I guess. That's all I can promise."

"That's all I'm asking. Thank you. There's something else, though," Lorraine said, finally opening the door. The dogs slithered past them to galumph around the front yard, tussling with each other in a whirlwind of leaves. "You remember what I said, about how you brought Ryder out of himself when he was a little boy?"

"Yes…?"

Concern softened Lorraine's features. "Deanna's death…it pushed him into a very dark place, Mel. Not so most people could tell, but I can. The moment you returned, though—"

"Oh, no, no—I know where you're going with this—"

"You could bring him back, Melanie. I know it, I can already see the change in him. And then…well. Who knows what the future might bring?" At Mel's eyeroll, she added, "You're a mother, too, you know what I'm talking about."

"Yes, I am. And I appreciate how much you want to see Ryder heal." Mel's eyes burned. "So do I, my heart bleeds for him to see how much he's hurting. But you can't possibly equate what happened when Ryder was five to what's going on now. No, Lorraine, I'm sorry…but it's not up to me or anyone else to bring Ryder 'back,' except Ryder. Which he and I have already discussed," she said when Lorraine's mouth popped open. "And if you're suggesting I manipulate his emotions just to, to patch together a family, even for Quinn's sake…"

Mel paused, took a breath. "I will sacrifice almost anything for my daughter, but no way in hell will I go there," she said, then finally wrenched herself out of Lorraine Caldwell's force field and walked out the door. Except by the time she got around to the driver's side door, she heard Lorraine call to her from a few feet away.

Thinking, *Oh, for pity's sake—what now*? Mel looked up, the older woman's crumpled expression at odds with the stately white portico she stood under.

"I know I'm the last person who should be giving advice," Lorraine said over the bay breeze whipping strands of red hair around her face. "Or at least, the last person you'd want to take it from. But what the hell." She stepped closer. "Don't be a fool, Melanie. Don't let the bad blood between us blind you to what could be a blessing. And for God's sake don't let your hatred of me keep you from loving my son."

For a moment Mel felt as though she'd been knocked off her feet by a fire hose. But she recovered enough to say, "Not to worry. Since it never has."

A slow, knowing smile spread across Lorraine's face. "Good for you," she said, then returned to the house, the dogs trotting loyally behind her.

Ryder gunned out of the clinic's parking lot, cursing the twenty-mile-an-hour speed limit along Main Street until he spotted Mel's Honda headed in his direction on the other side. He honked, catching her attention, then pointed toward a duo of vacant, angled parking spaces in front of the town's only decent—according to his mother—beauty shop, housed in a narrow brick building that matched the brick sidewalk in front of it.

Before she'd cut her engine he was around to her door, holding it open as she climbed out. Then he yanked her into his arms, because he wanted to, had to, even though the clashing emotions as a result nearly made him dizzy. And not in a fun way.

"Let me guess." Mel's voice was muffled against his chest. "You talked to your mother."

Ryder set Mel apart before she suffocated, getting a *What are you doing?* look in response. "Just got off the phone, was headed toward your place," he said, amending, at her raised brows, "Fine. April's place."

"Except April took Quinn to the bookstore," she said, nodding toward the quaint little shop down the block, tables of used books half blocking the paned storefront windows, before looking back at him.

A pointed silence ensued, the brisk air swirling around them infused with the scent of the thousands of chrysanthemums crowded into whiskey-barrel planters lining both sides of the five-block stretch.

"They're expecting you, I suppose?"

Another glance toward the shop. More pointed silence. Followed by a sighed-out, "Not really. I just thought, since…never mind." Then her eyes touched his. "But what about you? Don't tell me you left a dozen people sitting in the waiting room, wondering where the heck you are?"

Ryder smiled. Gently chafed her shoulders. "Slow morning," he said, wondering what he *was* doing, to be honest. "Dad can handle things for a little while." Then, finally, he let go to plant one palm on her car's roof. "You okay?"

She sputtered a short laugh. "Sure thing," she said, and Ryder glanced at the town square across the street, then reached for Mel's hand.

"Come on—"

"Ry, no, really, I'm fine, you need to get back to work—"

Ignoring her, he steered her through what passed for traffic this time of day—or any time of day, actually—and into the little park crowded with flame-tinged maples and oaks, toward a black wooden bench badly in need of a fresh paint job. He brushed off a stray crimson leaf and sat, dragging Mel down with him. Still holding her hand, it should be noted.

Which she let him hold, it should also be noted.

Then he sighed. "Well, *that* sure as hell didn't go according to plan." He faced her scowling profile, although whether the hand-holding had anything to do with that, he had no idea. A squirrel scampered toward them across the leaf-littered grass, tail twitching, then seemed to think better of asking for a handout and scampered away again. "I was supposed to be there. For the great confession."

"So you know? That she had a fling with my grandfather?"

"Not until this morning. And only after I dragged it out of her. How *did* you find out, anyway?"

"Dear old Nana left a paper trail," Mel said drily, finally reclaiming her hand to fold her arms over her stomach. "A letter of apology from your mother, to be exact. Blythe discovered it among a stack of papers dating back to colonial days."

Ryder leaned forward to clasp his hands between his knees. "Damn, honey. I can't imagine what you must've thought. Are probably still thinking."

"I'm still…processing. Yeah, it was a million years ago, but at least I now understand the bug up my grandmother's butt. I understand a lot of things I never did before." She paused. "Did your mother tell you the part about how she did what she did—about me and Quinn, I mean—because my grandmother held a metaphorical gun to her head?"

"Yes." Ryder straightened, took her hand again. It was cold. And a little rough. A hand that worked, that fed people. That, along with its mate, had touched and stroked and driven him insane with pleasure, he thought on a rush of heat. That had cupped his face as she'd looked deep into his eyes, tucking him inside her far more deeply than sex ever could. He hauled in a breath. "Do you believe her?"

"I don't know," Mel said on a rush of air. "And I can't exactly go to the source, can I?"

He gently squeezed her hand. Resisted lifting it to his mouth. "I can't believe you bearded the dragon in her own den."

Her soft laugh made his skin prickle. "It's called adrenaline. Act first, think later. But whatever. It's done now, nobody died, and somehow…" She frowned. "Quinn and I are coming to dinner tomorrow night. Still not quite sure how that happened."

"Mom said. She's also ridiculously pleased about it."

"That makes one of us."

"But I thought—"

"I can't help it, Ry, I can't simply slough off the last decade because your parents want me to. Which I told your mother. And yet—" she sighed again "—I keep thinking I need to tell Quinn. Before this dinner. Except whenever I actually picture myself doing it, I get sick to my stomach."

Ryder shifted on the bench to make Mel look straight at him, his hand on her knee. "And to paraphrase something a wise and very beautiful woman once said to *me,* you will tell Quinn when it feels right and not a moment before. Although considering how you stood up to the old gal, something tells me you'll do just fine."

Mel gave a weak laugh. "I don't have to live with your mother. Compared with my daughter? Lorraine is a cupcake."

"I find that hard to believe."

"Quinn carries her genes, remember?" Her mouth flattened. "Not to mention mine. Child is doomed, I tell you. As are the rest of us."

He smiled, as well, then released a breath. "There's one more thing. I'm calling Jeremy tonight. To have a little chat."

"Oh, Lord, Ry…"

"Has to be done, honey."

"I know, I know, you're right, but…yeesh."

"Wanna be in on the call?"

"Not even if you gave me my very own key to the Godiva factory."

Ryder chuckled, then said, "Any messages to pass along?"

"Yeah," she said after a moment. Or six. "That whatever comes next as far as your brother's concerned is up to Quinn. Not him, not your parents. Quinn. If she wants to meet him, I mean. Not that I'm pushing for that, believe me. But no more lies. No more pretending. And no more letting Mama save his sorry ass."

"That's my girl," Ryder said over his cell phone's vibration in his jacket pocket. A text from his father. "Ah. Guess things are getting a little clogged at the clinic."

"I'm sure. And I do need to catch up with the others."

They stood and headed back across the street, both of them with their hands in their pockets. Halfway across, however, Mel glanced up at him, almost shyly.

"Thanks."

"For dealing with my bone-headed brother?"

"Well, yes, that. But also…for being you. Being here."

"I always am, honey. Always will be. Watch out for that car—"

"Oh, for heaven's sake!" she laughed out. "I'm a big girl now. I even beard dragons in their dens, remember?"

They reached his car; Ryder beeped the RAV unlocked, opened the door. Which would be his cue to get in the car. To let her go. Instead, she'd gotten as far as a quivering-leafed ash tree a few feet away when he called out, "So you're sure you're okay?"

She turned, walking backwards. But not quickly. "Yes, Ryder, I'm fine—"

"But you call if you need anything. I mean it. Promise?"

"Promise. But I won't."

"Stubborn little minx, aren't you?"

"Minx?" She stopped, grinning, her bangs fluttering

in the breeze, and his heart kicked him in the ribs. Hard. "Who the heck says minx anymore?"

"A thirty-something dude who stole a certain young *minx's* romance novel when they were kids. And read it."

Mel screeched another laugh, then looked down at the ground for a moment before slowly retracing the few steps she'd just taken, something like apology replacing the laughter in her eyes. "I'm not being stubborn, Ry," she said quietly. "I'm being practical. I know you mean well, really. But Quinn and I...we'll face this together, and we'll face it alone—"

"*Why,* for God's sake? I'm *here,* honey. For both of you. Always will be."

"Of course you are," she said, her eyes steady in his. "On your own terms."

Ryder felt his brows slam together. "What's that supposed to mean?" Except he knew damn well what it meant, long before Mel stepped off the curb to lay a hand on his arm.

"You're the same terrific guy I always knew, okay? And I do know I can count on you. I do. At least as far as knowing you're always on my side, that you'd never knowingly hurt me, or betray my trust. And I have no doubt you'll be the best uncle ever to Quinn. But you know what?" She sucked in a big breath. "I need more than that. I need *real.* I need *now,* and I need forever. If not from you, then from someone whose heart still isn't entailed to someone else."

His mother thought secrets were a bitch? Yeah, well, so was the truth. Especially when it hits you upside the head like a cast-iron skillet. "You said you were okay with... last night," he said stupidly.

"And I was. Am," she said, her expression pleading. *Please understand. Please forgive me.* Except why on earth was *she* asking for understanding? For forgiveness?

"But being around you…" She lowered her hand to clasp his, squeezing tight. "A repeat performance is too damn tempting."

A moment passed before he said, very softly, "Can't argue with you there."

"And that, I wouldn't be okay with." One last squeeze, then she dropped his hand. "Not as things stand now. I *don't* regret last night. And I never will. But it took last night to make me realize…"

She smiled. Not the hero-worship smile of the "little sister" he once knew, but gonna-do-this-if-it-kills-me smile of an adult with the courage to make hard choices.

"Being back here did more than force me to face the past, it's also made me reassess who I am. What I really want. What I really *need*. And that, my sweet friend, is someone who is absolutely nuts about me, who loves me the way my father loved my mother. Hell, who loves me the way *your* father loves *your* mother." Her eyes filled. "Who loves me the way you obviously loved Deanna."

Cue the skillet, Take Two.

Ryder released a long, ragged breath. "Damn, Mel—"

"And you can stop right there. It's not your fault you can't be that person. But that's why I don't dare let myself count on you. Because I'm afraid I'll start seeing things that aren't there. That probably won't ever be there."

His throat working overtime, Ryder looked away to force out a humorless laugh. "The timing—"

"Sucks. I know. Hey. It happens."

He faced Mel again, lifting his hand to thumb away the wetness on her cheek. "How'd you get to be so damn amazing?"

"Copious amounts of bacon," she said, standing on tip-toe to kiss his cheek before walking off.

Chapter Ten

Standing with Mom in front of the blindingly white door with the shiny brass knocker, Quinn lifted one foot to scratch the back of her other leg through her new leggings. Which she loved, don't get her wrong—they were white with polka dots in every color you could imagine—but they were a little itchy. Not so bad that she couldn't deal, though. Besides, they looked totally awesome with her *also* new purple sweater and silvery ballet flats with the big bows across the toes, and anyway, Blythe said sometimes you had to suffer to look good. Mom had rolled her eyes at that. Blythe also said Quinn looked bitchin', but later, when Mom wasn't around.

"You ready for this?" Mom said, taking Quinn's hand, and Quinn thought, *Ready for what?* but she smiled up at her, anyway. Mom looked totally *bitchin'* tonight, too, in this amazing turquoise dress in some real soft fabric that made her look all curvy, with the cutest matching sweater with little beads scattered down the front. And high heels. *Really* high heels. With lots of straps crisscrossing the tops of her feet.

"Sure," she finally said, feeling like it was somehow up to her to make Mom feel better. Even though her mother's hand was cold and kind of damp—ick—Quinn didn't pull away. Because it was pretty obvious how nervous she was. Which Quinn guessed had something to do with Ryder. Again. Or still. She wasn't sure which.

She and April had come out of the bookshop yesterday right when Mom kissed Ryder on the cheek, and after he'd gotten in his car and driven away Mom had noticed them, smiling all fast like everything was good when *anybody* with half a brain in their head could see it wasn't. Then she'd suggested they all go to the outlet mall nearby, because she and Quinn had been invited to dinner at Ryder's parents' house and they could *not* go looking like a couple of bums, she said.

Instead of, for once, maybe actually talking about what had just happened? So, per usual, Quinn got a shopping trip instead of answers. Although, actually, the shopping trip was a new thing. Usually it was cookies. Sometimes a cake or pie, but usually cookies.

One thing was for sure—things hadn't gotten *less* weird over the last few days. Especially since she kept catching Mom staring at nothing with this not-really-there look on her face. Or frowning, like she was trying to figure something out. Or sighing. *Lots* of sighing. And every time Quinn would ask if she was okay, all she'd say was, "Sure, sweetie, why wouldn't I be...?"

"So, you gonna ring the doorbell?" Quinn asked, suddenly realizing how long she'd been standing there thinking about stuff. And that the wind was going right up under her little skirt and freezing her butt.

"Sorry," Mom muttered, and punched the button, the ding-donging making the dogs bark on the other side of the door. Quinn stepped back.

"Don't worry, they're harmless," Mom said, and Quinn wondered how she knew that.

Ryder's dad answered the door, smiling like always and telling both her and Mom how nice they looked. Then he gave Quinn a wink, which made her giggle. The dogs made her giggle, too, so excited to see her she could barely get inside the door.

"Lucy! Ethel! Come! Sit!"

At the sound of the woman's voice, the dogs stopped trying to lick Quinn's face and left to sit by the tall, thin, redheaded woman belonging to the voice. She was really pretty—for somebody that old, anyway—but not dressed up nearly as much as she and Mom were. Black pants and a long, kinda beigey sweater, a chunky gold necklace—that was it. Then she smiled at Quinn, her hand stretched toward her like they already knew each other, and *now* Quinn felt seriously funny inside, like she did know her from somewhere but couldn't remember.

"Quinn, sweetheart," she said, her smile getting brighter, like a light bulb right before it dies. "I'm Lorraine Caldwell. Ryder's mother."

"Nice to meet you," Quinn said, taking her hand, because she hadn't been raised by badgers, as her grandmother used to say, and Mrs. Caldwell said, "Very nice to meet you, too. And don't you look lovely!" and Quinn said, "Thank you, so do you," and she thought *Ohmigosh, this could go on all night.*

"And don't you have the nicest manners, young lady!"

Young lady? Brother. Then again, they were going back to Baltimore in a couple of days—which wasn't sitting all that well, truth be told—so what were the chances she'd ever see Ryder's mother again, anyway?

Then Ryder appeared out of nowhere and Quinn ran to him and he lifted her off her feet in a big hug, and suddenly she felt like crying for no good reason that she could tell.

All through dinner, Ryder could tell Mel was holding her breath as she picked at her food, clearly apprehensive that one or the other of his parents would let something slip. They wouldn't, of course, both well aware how easily this fragile truce could be blown. However, when his mother asked Quinn how she liked St. Mary's, he could practically hear Mel's hammering heart, her eyes wide and even darker than normal as she awaited Quinn's answer.

"It's okay, I guess," the child said with a shrug, her own gaze darting to her mother as though unsure what to say. Then she grinned at him and his heart melted. Again. "I like all the cute little shops and stuff. But mostly I like sitting out on the dock and watching the water and sky. And the birds," she said to his father.

"Are we still on for tomorrow?" David said, and Quinn looked at Mel, who hesitated before nodding, and Quinn did a fist pump, making his mother laugh. His mother. Laughing. At a fist pump. Honestly, Ryder felt as though he'd landed in an alternate universe.

One in which one stunningly beautiful Melanie Duncan was apparently loath to meet his gaze, which was bugging the life out of him. Well, except when he asked her to pass the rolls, and her gray-shadowed eyes had shot to his as though he'd suggested fencing stolen goods, and regret slashed at his gut, that what they'd had lay in ruins between them. That they'd somehow managed to wander into that limbo between friendship and *more,* where they simply didn't fit together anymore.

That here was this incredible woman saying, basically, *I'm yours for the asking,* and he...couldn't.

Can't? Or just too damn afraid?

"Let's have dessert in the living room!" his mother said, rising, sounding more chipper than Ryder ever remembered, and despite the lead weight in his stomach he smiled at how Quinn carefully folded her cloth napkin and laid it atop her empty plate before getting to her own feet, and he caught Mel's eye and winked—because he was perverse like that—making her blush.

Then, remembering, as the others drifted into the formally furnished room that hadn't been used since forever, he snagged her elbow and whispered, "We need to talk."

Her gaze zinged to Quinn, who'd already discovered the baby-grand Steinway by the bay window, her smile enormous when his mother encouraged her to go ahead and try it out, if she liked.

Mel bit her lip. "But—"

"They're not going to do anything stupid, Mel. Way too much at risk." He turned his head, lowering his voice even further. "I talked to Jeremy."

That got her attention. "When?"

"This evening," he said, steering her toward the two-story conservatory at the back of the house, the interior washed in coppery light from the rapidly fading sunset. "I'd called, left a couple of vague messages both on his home phone and cell, but he didn't get back to me until then."

"Oh." She left his side to meander through a virtual jungle of multicolored hibiscus, the trumpet-shaped flowers glowing like jewels, stopping to cup one magnificent coral blossom in her palm. "What did he say? When you told him why you'd called?"

"Not a whole lot. I got the feeling he couldn't talk freely.

Because he wasn't alone, I assume. But he knows. That the jig's up."

"And you told him—?"

"I did."

Mel dropped the flower to press her folded arms to her middle. "So. That's done, then."

"It would appear so." Ryder paused, then said, "I've never seen you in heels before."

Smiling slightly, she glanced down, turning out one foot to pose, then back up at him. "I have to admit, they're strangely…empowering."

"For you, maybe," he said, and she laughed, then shifted to look out over the gardens, a few valiant blooms defying the shorter nights and cooler temperatures.

"We should get back," he said, and she shuddered. Sighed.

"Probably."

Ryder slowly closed the distance between them to drape his arms around her shoulders and pull her close. Unresisting, she melted into him, and he ached. For her, for himself, for what couldn't be.

"So why wouldn't you look at me during dinner?"

She was quiet for a long moment, then said, very softly, "Because despite everything I said yesterday, there's this nasty little voice in my head that will not shut up. A voice that keeps telling me I could fix you." She paused. "Love you enough to heal your heart."

When he found his voice again, all he could say was, "Wow."

"I know, right?"

He chuckled softly into her soft, sweet-smelling hair. "That's incredibly…honest."

"And wrong, on so many levels." After another shrug, she twisted to look up at him. "I hurt so much for you, Ry.

More than I can even begin to put into words. And it slays me, that I *can't* make it better."

Feeling as though he was about to burst into flames, Ryder cradled the back of her neck and lowered his mouth to hers, the kiss soft and deep and bittersweet, before tucking her against his chest, whispering, "Yeah. Me, too."

Because it wasn't that he didn't love her—always had, always would.

It was that he didn't love her enough.

Dude was gonna kill her dead, no lie.

They stood for some time, cocooned in silence and each other's arms, as though they both knew that conversation was over. Not to mention the relationship. Only, see, that's what was driving Mel up a wall, that Ry so obviously wanted…something. To find his way out of his own head, if nothing else. And she could be that something, she knew it. Especially after that kiss. Because that kiss… it hadn't been about lust, and it sure as heck hadn't been about friendship. What it had been about, however, she had no clue.

And neither, she was guessing, did Ryder.

Except that he needed her. But if he couldn't see that, couldn't admit it, couldn't unshackle the pain and fear and grief that rattled and clanked along behind him, there wasn't a blessed thing she could do, was there—?

"So tell me something," he said, making her flinch, "did you put some kind of spell on Quinn before you brought her here tonight?"

Despite everything, Mel laughed. "Talk about a non-sequitur." Then she smiled up into that face she'd always loved, that somehow she'd known, even as a wee little thing, she'd love forever. In one way or the other. "You mean, the Stepford kid routine? That was my mother's doing," she said, forcing herself to let go, to distance herself from all that solidity and warmth and bone-deep goodness. "Since she said it never took with me, she was bound and determined to civilize Quinn. Kid knew how to use a twelve-piece place setting by the time she was five."

"Hmm. Almost as if—"

"She knew she'd need that particular skill someday. I know. Crazy, huh? Then again, I think on some level she understood a lot more than I gave her credit for. Or wanted to believe. Not just that she'd meet her other grandparents someday, but all of it. The *why* behind what happened."

"You mean, about your grandmother?"

"Yeah." Mel walked away to toy with the frond of an immense fern in a majestic, hand-painted urn, her insides pinching at how well Ryder understood *her,* even after all this time. "You know, I never understood my mother's unswerving loyalty to yours. Even after we left, she never, ever said a word against her. I thought she was nuts, frankly. But now...maybe I can see things a little differently. Not that part of me doesn't still wish your mother had stood up to my grandmother. Called her bluff. Because frankly I'm not sure Nana would have ever made good on her threat, never mind how much your mother *believed* she would."

She turned. "However, I've been thinking a lot the past couple of days, about how Mom was able to put everything that happened behind her and move on." Her throat got so tight she could barely get out, "Including forgiving me for screwing up her last chance at patching things up with her mother. While my grandmother hung on to her resentment and grudges every bit as tightly as she held on to all the crap in that house." She gave Ryder a small smile. "And I had to ask myself which example I'd rather emulate, for my own sake as well as Quinn's."

He smiled back. "So you're saying you'll never be a hoarder?"

"Oh, Lord, no," Mel said on a laugh. "But it also means I can't let the past deprive Quinn of something she wants. And needs."

"Sounds like a plan," Ryder said quietly, his features unreadable in quickly fading light. Then, his voice even softer: "Thank you."

Mel nodded, then glanced around the conservatory, the taller specimens ghostly in the near-dark. "We used to play hide-and-seek in here. Remember?"

A beat or two passed before he said, "You were, what? Four? Five?"

"Something like that, yeah." She forced a laugh past her still-clogged throat. "And you were a *such* a jerk, jumping out at me when I'd get close to finding you, making me scream."

"What can I say, I've always loved to make you scream."

Mel pushed out a fake sigh. "Now *how* did I know you'd say that?"

He sighed as well. A genuine one, in his case. "Innocence lost?"

"It *was* innocent, then. I always felt safe with you. Protected. And those memories…they can't be tainted. Can't be taken from us. Ever. I like that."

"Yeah," he said after a long pause. "Me, too."

"And you know something else?" Her eyes burned. "The more I think about the good stuff, the less important the bad stuff seems. And I *really* like that." When he didn't respond, she said, "We're leaving on Monday, by the way."

"Oh. So soon?"

Mel refused to hear disappointment in his voice. Or, far worse, hope in her own head.

"I'm actually holding off an extra day—so Quinn can have her birding adventure with your dad—but April's got things pretty much under control with the house, and, um, I've got three interviews lined up. And this one place, if it pans out—I could start immediately."

Another pause. Then: "So you really won't consider staying? To take April up on her offer."

She thought of that incredible kitchen-to-be, the chance to make up her own menus, to have something that was her own—

"I can't, Ry."

Silence. In the dark, she held her breath. *Your turn,* she thought, closing her eyes and feeling her heart hammering in her chest. *Give me a reason to stay—*

"Are you planning on telling Quinn before or after you leave?"

Tears crowded the corners of her eyes. She blinked them back. "At the moment I'm going with after. I think it'll be better, don't you? Give her a chance to assimilate things away from here. That way if there's fallout, nobody feels it but me. After the dust settles I'll get in touch with your parents, and we can take things from there, I suppose. But whatever happens, it's all about Quinn. Just like always."

If Ryder wondered about her sudden verbal spewage, he didn't let on. Instead he said, "Those stitches can come out in a couple of days," and she said, "Right, I'll see to it," and then he took her hand to lead her out of the dark, and by now treacherous to navigate, space.

They found his parents and her beaming, animated daughter playing Monopoly in the den, her initial shyness with Lorraine apparently dissolved. A quick glance at the board made Mel chuckle. Judging from the nice little stack of play money in front of the kid, clearly Quinn was beating the socks off her grandparents. Who were both, just as clearly, getting an enormous kick out of it. In fact, at Ryder's and Mel's reappearance, Lorraine looked up and smiled at Mel, her hand pressed to her heart as she mouthed, "Thank you."

Then the dogs, who'd been sacked out on the thick rug as close to Lorraine as they could get, both jumped to their feet and bolted from the room, barking. Mel barely caught Lorraine's exchanged glance with David, a frown marring her brow, before, muttering an obscenity, Ryder strode from the room.

Then she heard voices. Ryder's, of course, and a woman's she didn't recognize.

And a man's she did, even if lower than it had been ten years ago.

Her heart rocketing into her throat, Mel whipped around to face a very pale Lorraine as Mel heard Jeremy say behind her, "Well, isn't this convenient, everyone's here for our little reunion...."

This couldn't be happening. Couldn't—

Quinn's puzzled gaze swung to Mel's. "Mom—?"

"Mel, Quinn—" David beckoned them toward the French door leading outside. "Come on—"

But it was too late. There he was, a study in preppy chic trailed by the pretty Asian woman Mel had seen in the photo. Who looked every bit as befuddled as her husband looked determined, his rectangular-framed gaze latched on to Quinn.

"Hello, honey—you must be Quinn—"

"Please, Jeremy, don't," Mel said, her heart shattering, as Ryder grabbed his brother's arm.

"Don't be an idiot, Jer—"

"I'm Quinn, yeah," her daughter said, slowly getting to her feet, confused eyes darting between Mel and Jeremy, and Mel caught his wife's gaze in a frantic, silent plea, saw the horrified understanding dawn in them.

"Jerry, maybe this isn't—"

"Who are you?" Quinn asked.

"Jeremy!" Ryder boomed, at least distracting his brother long enough to allow Mel to grab Quinn's hand and yank her toward the door.

"Mom! What's happening? Ow! You're hurting me!"

"Stop!" Lorraine bellowed, stunning everyone into silence. "Jeremy, shut up and sit down. Mel and Quinn—" Her voice softened, she shut her eyes a moment, then waved them back into the room. "Since I caused the wreck—"

"Mother—"

One hand shot up to ward off whatever Ryder had about to say, but his gaze swung to Mel's as she stood behind Quinn, arms criss-crossed over her chest, feeling her daughter's rapid heartbeat underneath her hands.

Until Quinn wrenched free of Mel's clasp and headed toward Jeremy.

"Quinn!"

"It's okay, Mom. I've got this." Hands plunked on hips, she stared him down, and in that stare Mel saw, with a mixture of pride and sheer terror, all the women whose ballsy genes she carried. "You're my father, huh?"

Chapter Eleven

"Your mom really was going to tell you," Quinn heard Ryder say beside her as they walked along the shore, the moonlight making the marsh grasses look like thousands of wobbly silver spears.

"When she got tired of lying to me, you mean?" She tugged Ryder's way-too-big jacket up around her neck, even though the cold breeze felt good against her hot face. "And *please* don't tell me to calm down."

"Wouldn't dream of it." He paused. "It feels good to be mad, doesn't it?"

"Yeah," she said, except what it felt like, was like she had one of those marsh spears stuck right in the middle of her chest. After all this time of wishing Mom would talk to her, be honest with her, now when she should be talking to Mom…she couldn't. All she wanted was to be left alone. And how messed up was that?

Only, after she'd run outside, Ryder had followed her,

refusing to go away. A thought that tickled her brain in some funny way, but she did not have the energy to figure it out.

"Can I say something?" he said.

"Whatever," Quinn said, knowing she sounded bratty and not really caring.

"You're going to have to let your mother explain the details of what happened, how we all got to this point. Because," he said when Quinn opened her mouth, "she *is* your mother and she loves you more than life itself, that's why. She was also worried sick that this is exactly how you'd feel." Quinn punched the toe of her new shoe into the sandy dirt, probably getting mud all over it. "But you have to understand…she was pretty much forced to keep this all a secret. Until she realized how unrealistic that was. So she'd had a plan. Which was going fine, actually, until my dimwit brother showed up and shot it all to heck and back."

"Yeah, about that…" Quinn turned to Ryder. Who was her uncle, actually, a thought that had a hard time squeezing into what little space was left in her brain. "So this dude knows about me the whole time and just blows me off? And then comes back and expects me to…what? Act like everything's cool? And by the way, you can go ahead and swear, it's not like I've never heard it or anything."

"Noted," he said with a nod, then said, "I have no idea what Jeremy's thinking. But your mom told me a few days ago that it's entirely up to you, whether you want to get to know him or not. He gave up his rights ages ago, so he can't play that card now."

"So you knew all along, too?"

"Not all along, no. Only since you and your mother came back to St. Mary's." They walked for another few seconds before he said, "It's all very complicated, honey.

And trust me, your mother's hurting every bit as much as you are right now."

"So you're taking her side."

"There are no *sides,* Quinn," Ryder said, his voice a little sharp. "Right now you might not want to believe it, but it's true. And God willing from this point forward there won't be any more lies, either. That's the best any of us can do. You either deal with that or you don't."

They'd walked in a big circle and were now coming back to the house, making her insides hurt all over again. "Man, I cannot wait to go home. Back to Baltimore, I mean." Except even as she said it, that didn't feel right, either. Nothing felt right anymore. Quinn half wondered if it ever would.

"Going home with your mom?"

She felt her mouth twist. Along with her insides. "Guess I don't have a whole lot of choice in that."

"None that I can see. But you know, something tells me the two of you will work through this."

"I guess." There was this big porch that stretched across the whole back of the house, so you could go outside from several rooms. In the light from one of them she saw her mother standing. Watching for them, Quinn guessed. "Can I say something?"

"Anything you like."

"Two things, actually. One, thank you for not talking to me like I'm a baby."

"You're welcome—"

"And two…" Her chest all tight, Quinn looked up at Ryder, walking beside her with his hands in his pants pockets. "Why couldn't it've been you? To be my father, I mean?"

He got very quiet, then reached for her hand, holding it tightly as they got closer to the house. And she let him.

"Because I cared too much about your mother to go there," he said softly, which Quinn didn't entirely understand but she got the gist, as her grandmother used to say. "But I'll tell you what—if I were, I'd be the proudest man on the planet. You are one awesome kid. Just like your mom was, when she was your age."

Quinn thought that over a moment, then said, "Do you still think she's awesome?"

"You have no idea," he said, but she had to strain to hear him.

When they reached the bottom of the porch stairs, she threw her arms around Ryder's waist and hugged him, then ran up the stairs before he saw her cry.

Mel's mangled heart lurched into her throat when Quinn flew into her arms, nearly knocking the stuffing out of her.

"I'm sorry I got mad," she said, her voice muffled against Mel's stomach. She looked up, saw Ryder standing at the bottom of the stairs. He gave her a thumbs-up and a forlorn, and yet somehow proud, smile that brought tears to her eyes. Okay, *more* tears.

Then he walked away, back into the night, as if to say *My work here is done,* and Mel buried her face in her daughter's hair, thinking, *Just hell, that's what this is. Just bloody hell.*

"It's okay, you had every right to be upset—"

"Can we go home now? I mean, like tomorrow?"

"But you were looking forward to going birding with David tomorrow—"

"You mean—" Quinn's head arched back, hurt blaring in her eyes. "—my *grandfather?* You lied to me, Mom! You told me you didn't know where my father was—"

"And technically I didn't! And hey—" Clumsily lowering herself to her knees—damn shoes—Mel clamped her hands around Quinn's arms, hooking her daughter's gaze in hers. "You want to be angry with me, fine. But don't take it out on Dav— your grandfather—"

"Or your mother," Lorraine said, she and the dogs emerging from the den onto the porch. "If you want to blame anyone, blame me. Because as I said…this is all my fault. No one else's."

Then, with a heavy sigh, Ryder's mother sank onto a spiffy glider nearby, making it groan. Mel struggled to her feet—damn tight dress—and said, "Where's—?"

"Gone. To a bed and breakfast in town. Poor Caroline was appalled, for whatever it's worth." Mel saw Lorraine's gaze cut to Quinn, standing slightly behind Mel and holding her hand, then back to Mel. "I was just as blindsided as you. I had no idea Jeremy was coming. I swear. And I'm still not entirely sure why he did. What purpose he thought it would serve. Not that I'm not glad it's finally out in the open," she quickly added, once more addressing Quinn. "But this was a terrible way for you to find out. So from the bottom of my heart, I'm sorry. Will you…will you give me a chance to make it up to you?"

At her daughter's silence, Mel looked down and saw Quinn's mulish expression, then returned her gaze to Ryder's mother. "You've got your work cut out for you, Lorraine. Stubbornness running in the family and all."

Lorraine smiled—a small, tired smile—then said, "Then would you at least let me explain? Or try to?"

After several seconds, Quinn finally nodded, and Mel felt a burden she'd carried for way too long finally begin to slide off her shoulders.

Even if the burden didn't seem even remotely interested in taking the heartache with it.

* * *

Despite Lorraine's reasonably thorough explanation—and repeated apology—Quinn still insisted on going home the next day. She did allow David and Lorraine to come say goodbye—with a kitten as a going-away present, Lord help them both—but while the kid had been unable to say no to all that mewing, furry cuteness, she'd been less than committal about rescheduling her outing with her grandfather. Which Mel knew hurt David deeply, even though privately he'd said he understood. That she needed time.

And, after apologizing yet again, Lorraine had hugged Mel hard enough to squeeze whatever lingering resentment was left right out of her. Not that she was ready to call the woman her BFF or anything, but at least they'd laid enough issues to rest between them that Mel could envision future holiday get-togethers without getting twitchy.

Of course, that was all up to Quinn. Who, a week on, was still having a hard time dealing. And who sometimes only seemed to tolerate Mel's presence because otherwise she'd starve to death. Not surprising, Mel supposed as she dragged herself up the front steps to their row-house apartment after getting off work, there being no magic wands handy to wave over the past decade and make it disappear.

Not to mention that damn heartache that had ridden shotgun back from St. Mary's to insinuate itself in Mel's life like an obnoxious, freeloading roommate with no concept whatsoever of personal space. And who kept whispering that her new job—a job there was no reason she shouldn't absolutely love—sucked.

That being back in Baltimore sucked.

That having Ryder as a friend was better than not having any Ryder at all.

That—yet again—she'd screwed up.

The kitten attacked her Crocs, all black-and-white bodaciousness, and Mel scooped up the little purrpot to cradle him underneath her chin. From the living room she heard the *Househunters* theme—Mrs. Davis's fave HGTV show. The elderly woman was sawing logs, of course, although she jerked to attention when Mel plucked the remote off her lap to turn off the TV.

Muttering about how she'd just dozed off for a second, that Quinn had gone to bed an hour ago, she'd been an angel, as usual, she accepted Mel's gentle hug before giving the kitten a pat on the head and then leaving. On a sigh, Mel kicked off her shoes and padded in her socked feet to the kitchen to make herself some chai tea, only to jump when she noticed Quinn standing in the doorway in Target-issue jammies and her Angry Birds slippers. Fitting.

"Mrs. Davis said you were asleep."

"I was. Did you know the whole house shakes when somebody opens the door?"

Mel smiled. "I did. You want something? Hot chocolate? And I brought leftover cheesecake from the restaurant."

"Is it yours?"

"No, they have their own pastry chef."

"Then no. I'm not hungry, anyway. But I do want to talk."

"Oh?"

"Yeah." The birds glared at Mel as Quinn scuffled across the kitchen to drop into a chair, stabbing her hands through her tangled red mop. "And don't worry, I'm over being mad at you. I think. I'm just…confused."

Her tea made, Mel sat across from her daughter. "About?"

"Everything," she said on a dramatic sigh, letting her head flop back against the high-backed chair. "How I can be soooo mad at my…my grandparents and miss them at the same time." Her eyes lowered to Mel's. "How you could

act, like, everything's all fine after what they did to you. To us." Her mouth pulled into a tight little line. "Why you and Uncle Ryder can't see how crazy you are about each other, geez. I mean, *seriously.*"

Oh, dear Lord. Mel stared into her tea, sorely wishing it was something stronger. Like Pine-Sol, maybe, to disinfect her brain.

"Well, in no particular order… Did you ever hear the saying 'Fake it till you make it'?" Quinn nodded. "To be honest, when we first got to St. Mary's I was still extremely angry with the Caldwells. For what certainly seemed to be valid reasons. And I was pretty determined you'd never have a relationship with them."

Quinn's nose wrinkled. "Then how come you changed your mind?"

"A combination of things, I guess. Discovering far more of the truth than I knew before. Realizing how much it takes out of you, being bitter all the time. Angry. And it occurred to me I didn't want to be the kind of person who hangs on to the past like…like—"

"A gazillion old magazines?"

Mel snorted. "Yeah. But realizing something and making it happen are two different things. So I'm still a work in progress on that front. I do believe your grandparents mean well—now, anyway—and I want to believe your grandmother's had a change of heart. But I still get angry sometimes. Like you," she said, and Quinn lowered her eyes, her cheeks coloring. "However, the good news is that each time it has less of a grip on me than the time before."

Suddenly a light went on behind the kid's eyes. "Like the Cherokee wolf story?"

"Huh?"

"Yeah, it's…" One hand went up. "Hold on a sec."

The chair wobbled when Quinn jumped up and ran out

of the room, returning a minute later with a slim three-ring binder which she banged open on the table. "You made me write a report on it," she said, tucking her foot up under her tush as she flipped through the pages. "Here it is."

Cramming her hair behind her ear, she read: "'An old man tells his grandson that there are two wolves fighting inside him. One is evil—hate, anger, resentment, self-pity...' and so on," she said, circling with her hand, then continued, "'The other is good—kindness, love, serenity...'" Her finger skimmed the line until she said, with a pointed look in Mel's direction, "*Forgiveness.* Then the little boy asks which one will win, and the old man says, 'The one I feed.'" Her eyes lifted to Mel's. "So you decided to feed the good wolf, huh?"

Oh, dear God, she loved this kid so much it hurt. Mel grabbed a rumpled napkin from the table and blew her nose. "I guess I did," she said. "In any case I finally had to admit it wasn't right, or fair, to prejudice you against your grandparents. That whatever relationship you end up having with them is between you and them. I won't interfere, one way or the other."

Quinn smacked shut the notebook, then leaned back in the chair, her arms crossed high on her flat little chest. "So it's okay if I like them?"

"Totally okay."

Forehead crunched. "Even if I'm still mad?"

"That's okay, too. But everybody makes mistakes, honey. And I mean everybody. What's important is how you fix them. And what you learn from them."

Judging from Quinn's yelp, the kitten attacked one of the Birds. Her hair quivered as she leaned down to haul the wee thing to her chest, where it started purring like mad, the contented sound at odds with the pain in Quinn's voice when she said, "Like you and Jeremy?"

Damn.

Mel leaned closer to pet the kitten. An invitation, apparently, to teethe on her fingers. "And sometimes," she said, "even the most boneheaded mistakes result in something amazing."

Eventually, a tiny smile peeked out from behind the confusion. "Even when you want to trade me for a dumb model?"

"*Especially* then," Mel said, laughing, and Quinn bounced up to come around and wriggle onto Mel's lap, kitten and all. *Enjoy it while you can,* she thought, twining her arms around her daughter's waist and not even caring that the kid's hair tickled like hell.

"I really liked St. Mary's, too," she said. Cautiously.

"Then I don't suppose you'll mind going back for visits," Mel said. Also cautiously.

"Actually…" She shifted to look down at Mel, her face the picture of earnestness as the kitten gnawed on her hair. "Jack was telling me about his school, it's right there in town and it sounds really cool, and I was thinking maybe it's time I try being in a classroom setting again, anyway—"

Mel sighed. "Not an option, baby."

"But if you married Ryder…?"

"Oh, honey—that's not an option, either."

"Why not? The three of us…we'd be awesome together, don't you think?"

Ice-pick-to-the-heart time. "Probably so. But that's not the point. Quinn, listen to me—remember how you told me about Jack's cousin and his mother, in that accident? Ryder really loved Deanna, and he's still not over it. Not enough to…" She breathed out. "Yes, he cares about me—about you, too—but look what happened with Lance—"

"You mean, about how his girlfriend came back so he

broke up with you? Mom!" Still clutching the oblivious kitten, Quinn slid off Mel's lap. "Hello? Ryder's girlfriend *can't* come back, can she? Okay, that sounded really terrible, but still. Like, totally not the same thing."

"Like, it totally is. *He* may be free, but his heart isn't. And that's what counts. Quinn," she said when her daughter rolled her eyes, "believe me, it breaks *my* heart to see him so unhappy. But I simply can't put myself through that. Not again." She reached over to take Quinn's hand. "Or you."

After several more cog-spinning seconds, Quinn tromped over to the fridge and got out the cheesecake, anyway, lugging the foam carton over to the table and plopping down to pick off pieces with her fingers and shove them into her mouth. "You know, if somebody would explain to me," she said around a full mouth, "why grown-ups make everything so darn complicated, I could die happy."

Sing it, sistah, Mel thought with a gloomy sigh.

The old place was definitely rising out of the ashes, Ryder mused as he pulled up in front of Amelia's house. Already, wheat-colored siding replaced the colorless, decaying clapboard from before, the broken trim restored and repainted a soothing teal-green. The yard, however, was gouged and cratered and muddy, thanks to a slew of pickups and vans from April's having apparently hired every contractor within a fifty-mile radius.

In paint-smeared jeans and a flannel shirt that might've fit Paul Bunyan, she met him at the door.

"Ryder! What brings you here?"

"Mel told me they'd left my jacket here?"

"Oh, right. Come on in. Let me wash my hands real quick and I'll get it for you. Don't bother shutting the door behind you, people are coming and going too much to bother."

He followed her inside, nodding in appreciation at the changes taking place. Light flooded the dust-caked downstairs, thanks to new windows, a wall or two removed, and mountains of clutter banished. "Wow," he said over the shouts and banging and satisfying din of rampant demolition. "This is incredible."

"And we've barely begun," April yelled back. "Blythe assures me it'll be done by early December, but I'm not convinced. Take a gander at the drawings, they're tacked up on the wall over there. I tell you, that woman is a freaking genius."

To say the least, he thought as he scanned the elevations of the proposed kitchen remodel—quartz countertops and pale wood cabinets, bright, white beadboard and restaurant-quality appliances, including a fridge large enough to store a side of beef in, he thought with a smile.

And a six-burner stove and matching double ovens.

In pink.

"Pink?" he said when April returned.

"Of course," she said easily as she handed him his jacket. "Because you know how much Mel loves pink."

Ryder started. "She's coming back?"

"Well, I suppose that's up to you, isn't it?"

"Excuse me?"

April grabbed a half-empty water bottle off a battered radiator cover and took a long swallow, twisting the cap back on as she said, "You've got a choice, you know. And I don't think I need to tell you what that is."

"And you're butting in."

"Damn straight, sugar. But only because you obviously haven't looked in a mirror recently to see how pathetic you look. Long face and everything, mm, mm, mm. People are *talking,* Ryder. In case you didn't know—"

"And maybe I care too much about Mel to offer her only half of myself."

"Lord, men," the blonde said, then jabbed a finger in his direction. "And *there's* a sorry excuse if ever I heard one. Ryder..." She leaned forward. "You're not miserable because of the love you lost, you're miserable because of the one you let get away. The one you're afraid to go after."

And the demolition ruckus now sounded eerily like it was coming from inside his head. "You just want her to come back to work for you."

"Heck, yeah, I want her to work for me. That's a given. Especially after some of the ding-dongs I've interviewed? I wouldn't trust them to feed my dogs. Well, if I had dogs. Anyway. Quinn also needs to be here, with her grandparents. And you. In fact, I'm not sure Quinn might not need you even more than Mel does, but don't quote me on that. I am sure, however, that the person doing the most needing is *you.* Only you're being too much of a scaredy-cat to admit it."

"I'm not afraid, April—"

"Oh, yeah? Then prove it. Not to me. To Mel. And Quinn. But mostly? To yourself."

His heart throbbing under his rib cage, Ryder mumbled, "Thanks for the coat. The place looks great," and got his sorry hide out of there.

Except, if he was angry, it was only because April was right. That this past week had been hell without Mel, that there wasn't a damn thing standing between him and a second chance at happiness except himself. And, yes, fear. Of what, exactly, he wasn't sure. That he'd let Mel down somehow? That he'd lose her like he'd lost Deanna and have to go through the pain again?

Only…he had lost her, hadn't he? And this pain…it was every bit as bad as the grief. Worse, actually.

Because at least with Deanna, it hadn't been his fault.

Although he'd planned on going into the clinic to catch up on some paperwork, he instead found himself driving back to the house—funny, how he'd never, not once, called the place where he lived *home*—through yellowing fields and the occasional clot of trees, gloriously ablaze against a serene, infinitely blue sky…

You have a choice.

His breath left his lungs.

The leaves would return, the crops replanted. The sky was always there. Life, existence, being, whatever you wanted to call it…it never ended, did it? Changed, yes— that whole doors opening and closing thing—but it was never, truly over.

Unless a person believed it was.

You have a choice.

Ryder blew out a long, rough breath as it hit him that what he felt for Mel was only *selfish* if he chose not to share it with her. And how could he not, since…

Since…

Since so much of what he'd loved about Deanna, he realized as his heart tried to pound right out of his chest, he'd loved about Mel, first.

He never made it back to the house. Didn't need to, since the decision pretty much made itself. And at first he considered returning to April's to ask for Mel's address, until he remembered someone else who'd have it.

"Ryder!" his mother said when he walked into his parents' house. "What—?"

"I need—" He paused. "Mel—where does she live?"

Slowly, her lips tilted, before she went to her desk to open her address book and copy something onto a piece

of her stationery. When she returned, however, she handed
him a set of car keys as well as the address.

"Take the Prius," she said. "It gets better mileage."

It was nearly dark when, as Mel lugged the heavier of
the grocery bags the short walk back home—so much for
just needing a "few things"—she watched Quinn disappear around the corner ahead of her.

Then heard the shriek.

Her heart in her throat, she rushed to catch up, only
to nearly wet herself when she saw Ryder sitting on her
porch steps, one arm looped around her hugely grinning
daughter.

"You weren't home," he said, as if that made perfect
sense.

And Mel burst into tears.

Some hours later, Ryder breathed out a satisfied groan.
"That was incredible." He reached for her hand to kiss her
knuckles. "*You're* incredible."

Mel grinned. "And there's plenty more where that came
from."

"Lord, woman, give a man time to recuperate. I'm not
seventeen anymore, you know."

Laughing, Mel got up from the kitchen table to clear
their dinner plates. Quinn had bolted down her food as
usual and was in her room, reading. Except she'd given
Mel a thumbs-up behind Ryder's back as she left the room,
which made Mel smile all the harder now. "It was just roast
chicken and potatoes, for heaven's sake."

"There was nothing *just* about it." Ryder rose as well
to cart the rest of the dishes to the sink, only to slip his
arms around her waist from behind as she turned on the
water, and Mel thought she'd die from happiness. Heaven

knew there were a million details to iron out—fat chance of any real conversation with a hyper-excited ten-year-old commandeering the conversation—but it didn't matter. Because the instant Mel saw him sitting on her steps, she knew. That he'd come for her.

For them.

So the question was, were they both ready for everything that meant?

"Mm. Nice," Ryder murmured into her hair, then gently turned her around to kiss her.

"Even nicer," she said, and he chuckled, his eyes going all crinkly at the corners before he kissed her again, slowly, like they had all the time in the world. Except... "The water's running."

Ryder angled himself around her to turn it off. "Problem solved," he said, then tucked her head under his chin, holding her close. "I'm putting the house on the market."

Mel leaned back to plant her damp hands on his chest. "Really."

"Yep."

"But you loved that house. And all the work you put into it—"

"Deanna loved the house. Frankly I'd rather live in town. And the work...like you said, it was therapy." Then he linked his hands at the small of her back, smiled into her eyes and said, "Where do you keep the coffee?"

"In the fridge," she said, lightly smacking his arm before he released her. "So you're letting it go? Just like that?"

"Just like that," Ryder said, dumping the Trader Joe's blend on the counter. "Filters?"

She reached into the cabinet overhead and handed him one, a little thrill of delight swirling through her at the deliciousness that was watching this man go about something as mundane as making coffee in her kitchen. The coffee started, he opened his arms and she walked into them, where he whispered, "It's okay, it's all over now" into her hair, and she knew what he meant. Except then he said, "Mom said she'd told you that Amelia never knew about our friendship."

Mel's head popped up. "She didn't." Then she frowned. "Did she?"

"I'm pretty sure she did."

"But how—?"

"Who knows? Maybe I left something of mine there when we were kids? In any case, I went out there to check up on the old girl once when Dad was busy, and she asked me if you were okay."

"You're kidding? When was this?"

"Maybe a month before she died?"

A jolt went through Mel. "And what did you say?"

"The truth—that I hadn't seen you in years. And she got this really shrewd look on her face, like she was processing the information." He tugged her close again. "Weird, huh?"

"Yeah," Mel said, her mind going a mile a minute. Speaking of processing information—

"By the way," Ryder said after several seconds had passed, "I'm staying in the old cottage. Until the right place comes along. Is that okay?"

Her heart jumped. "Of course—"

"I mean…" He cleared his throat, then set her apart enough to fish a ring box out of his pants pocket. "Would *you* be okay with living there?"

Wait. What?

"Holy crap, I need to sit," she said, grasping for the nearest chair and letting Ryder lower her into it, before lowering himself to one knee, his grin as unsteady as her legs.

"Ohmigod, Ry…are you sure?"

"Completely." He opened the box. Oooh, sparkly. "This is probably the weirdest proposal ever, but hear me out, okay?"

Struck mute, she could only nod. Ryder set the box on the table and took her hands in his, his eyes shiny. "Baby… I thought you were gone from my life forever. That what we'd had…that it really had been just some childhood thing I needed to let go of. But not until I finally felt free—and believe me, it took a helluva long time—did Deanna appear. And I loved her with all my heart, I truly did. Then, when she…went, I thought, that's it. Not going through that a third time. Except…inexplicably—" Poor guy looked so baffled Mel had to smile through her own tears. "There you were. Back in my life, under the most *extraordinary* circumstances. And all I could think was, what the hell?"

Mel burbled out a laugh, only to bite her lip when Ryder gripped her hands harder. "Fix me, sweetheart. Do whatever it is you do, I'm putting myself in your hands. Because whatever magic you worked on me when you were born, it's still working."

Took a second. "Ohmigosh," she gasped, her eyes wide. "You knew—?"

"I was five, Mel, well aware something was wrong with me. Just as I knew, even if I didn't understand how or why, that being with you released something inside me. Same way it is now. I know what I said, about the timing being all wrong, but…" He smiled. "It actually couldn't be more perfect, could it?"

Her eyes flooded, Mel shook her head, and Ryder finally retrieved the little box, slipping the pretty little pink diamond from its satin bed. "I know what I'm asking of you—"

"Yes," she said, wiping her eyes. Laughing. Sliding off

the chair to throw her arms around his neck. "Yes, and yes, and yes. To all of it."

"Then give me your hand, woman."

So she did, admiring the ring as Ryder said, "April will be beside herself—"

"She's not the only one!" Quinn said from the doorway. With a bark of laughter, Ryder opened his arm to include her in their first official, we're-a-family-now group hug.

And Mel thought, grinning, *Over? Like hell.*

Because the best part was just beginning.

* * * * *

REQUEST YOUR FREE BOOKS!

2 FREE NOVELS PLUS 2 FREE GIFTS!

❖ Harlequin

SPECIAL EDITION

Life, Love & Family

YES! Please send me 2 FREE Harlequin® Special Edition novels and my 2 FREE gifts (gifts are worth about $10). After receiving them, if I don't wish to receive any more books, I can return the shipping statement marked "cancel." If I don't cancel, I will receive 6 brand-new novels every month and be billed just $4.49 per book in the U.S. or $5.24 per book in Canada. That's a saving of at least 14% off the cover price! It's quite a bargain! Shipping and handling is just 50¢ per book in the U.S. and 75¢ per book in Canada.* I understand that accepting the 2 free books and gifts places me under no obligation to buy anything. I can always return a shipment and cancel at any time. Even if I never buy another book, the two free books and gifts are mine to keep forever.

235/335 HDN FEGF

Name _____ (PLEASE PRINT)

Address _____ Apt. #

City _____ State/Prov. _____ Zip/Postal Code

Signature (if under 18, a parent or guardian must sign)

Mail to the **Reader Service:**
IN U.S.A.: P.O. Box 1867, Buffalo, NY 14240-1867
IN CANADA: P.O. Box 609, Fort Erie, Ontario L2A 5X3

Not valid for current subscribers to Harlequin Special Edition books.

Want to try two free books from another line?
Call 1-800-873-8635 or visit www.ReaderService.com.

* Terms and prices subject to change without notice. Prices do not include applicable taxes. Sales tax applicable in N.Y. Canadian residents will be charged applicable taxes. Offer not valid in Quebec. This offer is limited to one order per household. All orders subject to credit approval. Credit or debit balances in a customer's account(s) may be offset by any other outstanding balance owed by or to the customer. Please allow 4 to 6 weeks for delivery. Offer available while quantities last.

Your Privacy—The Reader Service is committed to protecting your privacy. Our Privacy Policy is available online at www.ReaderService.com or upon request from the Reader Service.

We make a portion of our mailing list available to reputable third parties that offer products we believe may interest you. If you prefer that we not exchange your name with third parties, or if you wish to clarify or modify your communication preferences, please visit us at www.ReaderService.com/consumerschoice or write to us at Reader Service Preference Service, P.O. Box 9062, Buffalo, NY 14269. Include your complete name and address.

HSE11B

Sometimes love strikes in the most unexpected circumstances...

Soon-to-be single mom Antonia Wright isn't looking for romance, especially from a cowboy. But when rancher and single father Clayton Traub rents a room at Antonia's boardinghouse, Wright's Way, she isn't prepared for the attraction that instantly sizzles between them or the pain she sees in his big brown eyes. Can Clay and Antonia trust their hearts and build the family they've always dreamed of?

Don't miss

THE MAVERICK'S
READY-MADE FAMILY

by Brenda Harlen

Montana
★ MAVERICKS®
BACK IN THE SADDLE

Available this October from Harlequin® Special Edition®

*What happens when a Texas nanny learns she is
the biological daughter of a prince? Her rancher boss
steps in to help protect her from the paparazzi, but who
can protect her from her attraction to him?*

Read on for an excerpt of
A HOME FOR NOBODY'S PRINCESS
by USA TODAY *bestselling author Leanne Banks.*

Available October 2012

"This is out of control." Benjamin sighed. "Well, damn. I guess I'm gonna have to be your fiancé."

Coco's jaw dropped. "What?"

"It won't be real," he said quickly, as much for himself as for her. After the debacle of his relationship with Brooke, the idea of an engagement nearly gave him hives. "It's just for the sake of appearances until the insanity dies down. This way it won't look like you're all alone and ready to have someone take advantage of you. If someone approaches you, then they'll have to deal with me, too."

She frowned. "I'm stronger than I seem," she said.

"I know you're strong. After what you went through for your mom and helping Emma to settle down, I know you're strong. But it's gotta be damn tiring to feel like you've always got to be on guard."

Coco sighed and her shoulders slumped. "You're right about that." She met his gaze with a wince. "Are you sure you don't mind doing this?"

"It's just for a little while," he said. "You mentioned that a fiancé would fix things a few minutes ago. I had to run it through my brain. It seems like the right thing to do."

HSEEXP1012

She gave a slow nod and bit her lip. "Hmm. But it would cut into your dating time."

Benjamin laughed. "That's not a big focus at the moment."

"It would be a huge relief for me," she admitted. "If you're sure you don't mind. And we'll break it off the second you feel inconvenienced."

"No problem," he said. "I'll spread the word. Should be all over the county by lunchtime. No one can know the truth. That's the only way this will work."

Coco took a deep breath and closed her eyes as if preparing to take a jump into deep water. "Okay" she said, and opened her eyes. "Let's do it."

Will Coco be able to carry out the charade?

Find out in Leanne Banks's new novel—
A HOME FOR NOBODY'S PRINCESS.

Available October 2012 from Harlequin® Special Edition®